# Miles to Go

## Connie Bailey

Dreamspinner Press

Published by
Dreamspinner Press
4760 Preston Road
Suite 244-149
Frisco, TX 75034
http://www.dreamspinnerpress.com/

Miles to Go

Cover Design by Mara McKennen

ISBN: 978-1-935192-39-8

Printed in the United States of America
First Edition
December, 2008

eBook edition available
eBook ISBN: 978-1-935192-40-4

To J.M. McLaughlin,
Thank you for everything.

# ~ Chapter One ~

RICK'S ex-wife had often told him that he had some sweet moves, and he used all of them now to impress his audience. With a swagger that said he owned every inch of ground under his boots, Rick strutted across the nighttime city street to the Diesel Den. His leather jeans fit without a wrinkle, hugging his every nook and cranny, displaying his well-packed crotch in a blatant invitation to sin. A leather vest bared his broad, golden-furred chest, sculpted abs, and flat belly. With one pierced ear and a carefully chosen bandanna hanging from his hip pocket, Rick was a walking mating call for a particular breed of male.

The exact species, in fact, that inhabited the Diesel Den. The bar near the Greyhound station was a notorious hangout for the leather crowd, men who liked their sex with a rougher edge, who spoke of their love lives in code: B/D, S&M, Dom/Sub, etc. Rick knew he would find what he sought here and, wielding attitude like a sword and shield, he sauntered through the door as if the bouncer didn't exist. Only lost tourists stopped in foyers to gawk; Rick kept moving as if he walked in here every night at the same time. He took in the scene without being obvious about it: a long bar to his left, open space directly in front of him, and a smaller bar in the back right corner with a scattering of tables around a minuscule dance floor.

Rick glanced to his left as he headed for the front bar and spotted the short hallway that led to the restrooms. He saw a public phone and two doors marked Men and He-Men that preceded a larger door with an exit sign glowing red above it. Having memorized the topography and possible emergency exits, Rick signaled the bartender. The shaven-headed man brought Rick's beer and accepted his money without any drama. Taking a long swallow from the bottle, Rick turned his back on the bar and leaned against it. Now he had a perfect view of the place, and it didn't take long to spot his quarry. This was definitely the man Rick wanted, but the prey wasn't alone.

Rick stole surreptitious looks at the two bruisers flanking his target. Heavy musculature embellished with tattoos strained the fabric of their plain white T-shirts and well-worn Levis. Their hair was cut close to the scalp and their piercings would have set off a metal detector even without the handguns carried openly in shoulder holsters. Deciding the pair was no more intimidating than your average brace of attack-trained Rottweilers, Rick pushed away from the bar and paraded across the floor. Stopping in front of the back booth, he finished his beer in one long swallow and set the bottle on the table. The two large men got to their feet and loomed over Rick.

In contrast to the bodyguards, the man that remained seated wore a charcoal suit over a crisp white shirt and striped tie that would have made him presentable in the House of Lords. Like royalty granting an audience, the sharp-dressed guy deigned to look at the intruder and the illusion of urbanity was shattered. He might be wearing Savile Row's finest, but no trappings, no matter how elegant or well tailored could disguise the powerful frame of a street brawler. Rick gazed calmly back and let the man study him. He wasn't vain, but he'd been told that he was handsome often enough that he finally believed it. The gel-spiked hair wasn't his normal style and he rarely wore an earring these days, but he had dressed to attract the notice of a certain type of man. So far, it seemed to be working just fine.

Gareth Carey, known as "Hairy Carey" behind his back, stared at Rick in cold appraisal. At any moment, he could have the trespasser thrown out onto the street, but the brash golden stud intrigued him enough to stay his hand for now. His chilly eyes flicked toward his soldiers, Levere and Epiphano, in a subtle signal. Aside from sheer muscle mass and unchecked aggression, what set Gareth's men apart was their sexual orientation. The self-styled crime lord preferred to hire only gay men. It wasn't because he was gay; he still wasn't quite sure which category he fit into, but he believed homosexuals were less easy to tempt into disloyalty. He was probably fooling himself, but it brought him some badly needed peace of mind.

"What are you looking for, mate?" Gareth's British-accented voice was as smooth and rich as hot fudge. "Lost your top?"

Rick's easy smile betrayed none of his nervousness. "You like to get right to the bottom of things, don't you?"

"Cheeky," Gareth said without a smile. "But you're stalling, Blondie."

It was at about this point that Rick had planned to piss Gareth off and make hamburger out of his bodyguards, thus proving Rick's worthiness to replace one of them. He noted the relative positions of the thugs, his muscles tensing in preparation for a fight, but before he could crudely suggest that Levere and Epiphano's duties included bending over for their boss, he was interrupted. The most beautiful

3

man Rick had ever seen stormed up to the table and slid into the booth next to Gareth. Gareth pulled the pouting newcomer closer with an arm around his shoulders, but his gaze never left Rick.

"Maybe it's not a good time to talk business," Rick said, as Gareth's big hand settled on the newcomer's midsection.

A good two inches of fawn skin showed between the hem of the young man's tight red T-shirt and slim-cut black pants. Gareth's fingers spread across the dimpled belly button, the beginning of a dark treasure trail and a tribal style tattoo that led the eye downward. Rick quickly dragged his gaze back up to meet Gareth's and the other man's lips drew back in something that looked like a grin. Rick saw it for what it really was: an alpha male baring his fangs at a rival, establishing his territory. Rick smiled back in his best aw-shucks manner.

"Sorry if I was staring," he said. "But, shit, that's the prettiest guy I've ever seen."

"Billy," Gareth prompted. "That was a compliment."

"I hate Eddie Vane," Billy said loudly.

Gareth's eyebrows rose at the non sequitur. "What has our bartender done to earn your wrath, my red angel?"

"He won't serve me. He says I've had enough to drink for tonight."

Rick agreed with the bartender. Billy had definitely had enough to drink. The kid's big dark eyes were slow to focus and his posture had the boneless quality peculiar to career drunks and drowsing felines.

"I think Eddie Vane is right, tiger kitten," Gareth said. "Why don't you take a break?"

"Of course, Eddie Vane is right," Billy said, sitting up straight. "Eddie Vane is never wrong. That's not the point. Don't you get it? He refused to serve *me* and I'm with you. Everyone knows I'm with you; you made such a point of it. Is a light coming on in your brain yet?"

Gareth's gaze flicked up to his bodyguards again. "By refusing to serve you, Eddie Vane is disrespecting me. Is that your point, my damaged doll?"

"Well...duh," the young man responded. "Are you going to kill him?"

"I'm not really sure Eddie deserves to die," Gareth said. "Suppose I have him fired?"

"Fine," Billy said. "Whatever. If that's what your pride is worth, by all means have him fired."

"Baby," Gareth said reasonably. "You love Eddie Vane."

Billy sighed dramatically. "Again, you're missing the point."

Gareth gestured to Levere. "Tell Eddie he's fired. Give him the usual bonus and get Paul to come up front and tend bar. And for fuck's sake, get Billy a drink."

Levere moved off after shooting a final glare at Rick, and Billy appeared to notice the stranger for the first time.

"Who's this guy?"

"Rick Miller," Rick said. "I'm looking for work."

"Is that so? What do you do?"

"I keep bad things from happening to naughty little boys."

Billy turned to Gareth. "I like him. You should hire him."

"So you'd say he's got good qualifications, would you?" Gareth asked.

Billy gave Rick a hot-eyed look from under his unruly bangs. "He's the shit," the young man said.

"Well, Rick," Gareth said. "If you're willing to pass an audition and a background check, I would say your prospects are good. I like your references."

"You shouldn't try to be clever, Gareth," Billy remarked. "It doesn't suit you."

"Lambie," Gareth said, taking Billy's chin in his hand. "Let's not get personal."

Billy sobered before Rick's eyes, and fastened his earnest gaze on Gareth.

"Sorry, Gareth. That was thoughtless of me," Billy said contritely.

"You've got fire, Billy," Gareth said. "And I love it, but I don't like getting my whiskers singed in public."

"Public?" Billy laughed, pulling away. "Rick's practically family."

Gareth caught the young man's wrist as Billy slid out of the booth. "Where are you going, my bar butterfly?"

Billy laughed again and shook a finger in Gareth's face. "I promised this dance to someone else," he said.

Gareth let Billy go and watched the lithe figure sway onto the dance floor. Rick was careful to be looking elsewhere when Gareth's attention returned to him.

"Rick," Gareth said. "Do you know where I live?"

"Of course I do. I've planned this meeting for weeks," Rick said truthfully.

"I thought as much. You get points for balls. Be at my house tomorrow at eleven. We'll have breakfast, and talk, and then you can show me what you've got."

"Breakfast at eleven?"

"Call it brunch if you like, but Billy doesn't like to wake up early, and I like to do the waking, if you know what I mean."

"Can't say as I do, Mr. Carey," Rick answered. "Maybe someday I'll have the pleasure."

Gareth scowled. "Billy may like your cheek, but I don't. And don't call me Mr. Carey; call me Gareth."

"Gareth," Rick repeated. "Got it. I'll see you tomorrow, Gareth."

"Stay and enjoy yourself," Gareth offered. "You'll never pay for another drink in here."

"Or you'll fire the bartender," Rick couldn't help saying.

Gareth sat back, laying his arms along the top of the booth. "In a couple of days, Eddie Vane will be behind the bar again and Billy will pretend it never happened. Meanwhile, I've had to shell out a five-hundred-dollar bribe so my best bartender can enjoy some unexpected days off and my boyfriend will be sweet to me."

7

"Is it worth it?" Rick asked curiously, as Levere returned.

Gareth considered for a moment. "Yeah. It is."

Rick nodded. "Fair enough. I'll say good night, then; I'll need my rest for tomorrow."

Rick walked out of the Den without looking back at the booth. He caught a glimpse of Billy dancing with another supple young thing almost as pretty as he was. Rick ignored the hot pulse of lust that turned his deprived loins to lava. Nothing could come of it, and anyway, it was just two young men dancing. Just two beautiful, graceful, obviously aroused young men sliding and bumping against each other to the driving beat. Rick resolutely pushed the enticing image from his head and stepped out the door. He'd reached the end of the block when he noticed the car following him. Turning down the next side street, he slowed his pace. The car that was tailing drew alongside and stopped and the passenger door swung open. Rick got in.

"Howdy, partner," Officer Frederick "Rick" Miles said, as he buckled his seat belt. "Care to congratulate a man who's about to be employed?"

Rick's partner squealed and then turned it into an awkward cough. "That's fantastic, *hermano*. I never doubted you, of course. In fact, I defended you to…"

"Save it, Gracie," Rick said. "Once Marcial vouches for us, we're in up to our knees."

Sergeant Graciela Cruz grinned at her partner in unbridled glee. "I can't believe you knew High-Tone Marcial when he was in juvie, but it sure comes in handy now. Tonio must owe you big to do you this kind of favor. If his fellow dealers found out, *ay, eso chingado*; he'd be pretty fucked, *hombre*."

"Then we'll make sure they don't find out. Anyway, Tonio wouldn't mind if Carey went away on a more or less permanent basis."

"*No es mierda!* We'll show that Limey *cabron* he can't just set up shop on our side of the Atlantic. We'll take him down proper. Then they'll stop laughing at us."

"They laugh at us?" Rick asked with exaggerated innocence. "Who?"

"Stop playin' with me, Miles," Graciela said. "The whole precinct laughs at us. A Latina and a homo? Are you kidding? They call us Beanie and Weenie."

"I really don't see how that could be construed as offensive, Officer Cruz," Rick began, before she put a hand over his mouth.

"Just tell me how it went," she said. "Man, I still can't believe you waltzed in there without a wire and only me for backup."

"We've discussed all that, Gracie. We need to keep this simple, and it's over now anyway."

"No way, *hombre*," Graciela said. "It's just starting. So is Hairy Carey as sexy close up as he is through a long lens?"

"He's sexy as all hell," Rick said. "And mean as a snake."

"Yummy," Graciela said. "My favorite flavor. But go on."

"Everything went almost exactly the way you thought it would," Rick said. "It was a good plan, Gracie."

"Thank you," she took an awkward bow from behind the steering wheel.

"There was just one thing we hadn't counted on. Somehow we missed the fact that Mr. Gareth Carey already has a boyfriend."

"Shut up!"

Rick shook his head. "I met him. He ruined my pitch, and then told Carey to hire me."

"Shut! Up!"

"I'm crapping you negative, *chica*," Rick said. "That's how it went down. This is going to work; the angels are on our side this time. We'll find out when the next shipment is due and we'll catch Carey red-handed."

"And then we call the DEA," Graciela said.

"You got that right," Rick said, high-fiving her. "Then and only then do we call the Feds. They had their chance at this asshole in New York; now it's our turn."

"The nerve of this tea-suckin', left-side drivin', metric-system usin' Monty comin' over here with his big stiff upper lip tryin' to muscle in on our local purveyors of recreational pharmaceuticals. What's the world comin' to, *esai*?" Graciela said.

"You and me, Gracie," Rick said. "We'll make a better world, one scumbag at a time."

"You got that right," Graciela drawled in imitation of Rick's laid back California accent. "Let's go get a beer. Whatta ya say? *Cervezas frio* at your favorite cop bar?"

"Sure. Just let me change before we hit the Ten Forty-Two," Rick said.

Graciela snorted. "You're taking all the fun out of it, *pendejo*."

# ~ Chapter Two ~

"RICK. I'm glad you could come. Please sit down."

Rick looked down the long terrace at the back of Carey's mansion. Gareth half-rose from his padded wicker chair and gestured toward another on the other side of the glass-topped table. Rick sat and a brown-skinned woman set a well-laden plate in front of him.

"*Gracias, anciana,*" Rick said softly, making the old lady smile as she retreated.

Gareth looked curiously at Rick. "You speak Spanish," the Brit said.

"It's a good idea to learn some if you intend to live in SoCal," Rick said.

"Southern California," Gareth translated. "I've learned that one. Well, go ahead and tuck in if you're hungry."

Rick picked up a piece of cantaloupe. "I don't see any guards," he said. "Do you feel that secure here?"

Gareth nodded. "Once you're officially hired, you'll get the tour of the facilities and see all of the wonderful people and machines that keep the world out there at a comfortable remove. Right now, I want to have some breakfast and a small chat. Coffee?"

"The orange juice is fine," Rick said, looking around. "Very nice place you have, by the way."

Both men looked down from the patio at the sweeping grounds bordered by a high wall. A large deck below the terrace encircled a pool that gleamed like the world's largest piece of turquoise. A tanned body knifed through the sparkling water, turned at the wall, and swam resolutely back toward the other end. Epiphano stood at the edge looking like a bronze statue of an athlete from the first Olympic Games, if you ignored the Speedo. Rick glanced aside at his potential boss, but Gareth's gaze was fastened on the pool as Epiphano reached down a hand and hauled the swimmer from the water. The sun sparkled on the droplets that dewed the smooth skin, accenting the long, hard muscles of the trim physique, and Rick recognized Billy. As the young man reached for a towel, he shook the wet from his hair, spraying Epiphano.

"It's not much, but it's home," Gareth said, watching Billy walk up from the lower deck.

"He really is a knockout," Rick said. "Been together long?"

Gareth turned to look at Rick. "Were you this familiar with your last boss?" he asked sternly, before breaking into a smile. "I'm just taking the piss with you, mate. As long as you're respectful, you can ask me anything you like. You might not care for the answers you get, but you're welcome to ask."

"Have you and Billy been together long, Gareth?" Rick asked.

Gareth's smile broadened. "Persistent. I like that. No, Billy and I haven't been together long, though we've traveled in the same circles for a while. I imported him rather recently. A little taste of home, if you know what I mean."

Rick grinned. "Sweet, yet spicy."

"I can't stomach sissies," Gareth said. "And that boy drew blood the first time we kissed."

"Are you talking about me?" Billy asked, blocking the sun as he stopped in front of the table.

"What else would we be talking about?" Rick asked. "After the show you just put on."

Billy draped his towel over a chair, but didn't sit. "If this much skin embarrasses you, I can put more clothes on."

"It doesn't embarrass me," Rick said, eyeing the translucent white micro-thong Billy was almost wearing. "It embarrasses you. Though, I must say, a brown butt is a very nice sight."

Gareth looked up at his speechless lover like a sailor searches the sky for signs of bad weather. "I think you've met your match, my salty crumpet," Gareth said. "If Rick's as good with his fists as he is with his tongue, he's hired on the spot."

Billy looked down at Gareth through his lush lashes and gave the man a halfhearted pout before abandoning the ploy in mid-expression. Instead, he picked up the pitcher of orange juice and poured a glass. After taking a long swallow, he stared at the drink as if insulted. "I can't even taste the alcohol," he said.

"There's no alcohol in it, tiger kitten."

"Why not?"

"Try the bar, my lusty lamb, or the liquor cabinet. I'm sure you'll find something," Gareth said, smacking Billy's rock-hard glutes. "Rick and I have some business to finish up."

"Are you going to make him fight Levere? Or Epiphano?" Billy asked.

"What do you care?"

"I don't; just wondering which one of your attack dogs is going to the emergency room."

Gareth looked at Rick, but spoke to Billy. "You have a lot of confidence in someone you only met last night."

"I've seen his sort before," Billy said. "It's something in the eyes, something that shines like steel."

"Go on then, my poetic little fortune-teller, and have your drink," Gareth said, with an edge of something like steel in his voice. "And don't go out. I'll want to see you after we've put Rick through his paces."

Billy's face went utterly still for a brief second before he turned and walked away. Gareth was looking at Rick and didn't notice. Rick wasn't sure he'd seen it himself, it was gone so quickly, but he got the impression that the young man wasn't exactly thrilled at the prospect of a post-fight visit from his.... Rick wasn't sure what to call Gareth: lover, sugar daddy, pimp?

"Are you finished eating, Rick?" Gareth asked.

Rick nodded. "I'm ready."

"Good," Gareth said.

Rick saw the man's eyes change and some sixth sense sent him sideways out of his chair, dodging the surprise attack. Scrambling up from the flagstones, he faced Epiphano. Epiphano rose from the wreckage of the table with a crepe stuck to his massive bare chest and met Rick's charge. Rick hurtled into the muscle man, intending to take him down as quickly as possible. It worked better than he'd hoped. Epiphano put his foot down on a piece of china that skidded out from under him. The big man flew backward and tumbled down the steps with Rick wrapped around him. Locked in an inimical embrace, the two men hit the lower deck and broke apart. Rick rose first and delivered a roundhouse kick to Epiphano's jaw that sent the big man flying into the water. Gareth came down the stairs behind them, laughing heartily as he applauded.

"Enough," the Brit said. "You've proven that you can take care of yourself."

"It's the steely-eyes thing," Rick said. "My secret weapon."

Gareth laughed again. "Bloody hell, mate, you've got reflexes like I've never seen. What a fucking brilliant boxer you'd make. You might be interested in the local bare-knuckle tournaments. Fierce wagering. Bit of cash to be made there."

"I'll think about it," Rick answered, as he warily watched Epiphano climb out of the pool. "Can I assume my references checked out okay?"

"Marcial's people say you're *un macho*, which Billy assures me is the same as a righteous dude and a stand-up guy," Gareth said. "I'm not certain of all the connotations, but I assume it's a good thing. I'm sure you're aware that I'm the new lad in town and that I took this

16

territory from someone else. The turf war is over now, and I need solid people to help me build my empire. You have to decide your own level of commitment."

"What are you offering me?"

"You can be a soldier like Epiphano, Levere, Macross, and the other lads that do the heavy lifting, or you can be a lieutenant. You'll have to start as muscle, of course, but I think you're too smart to spend much more time breaking heads."

"I'll think about that, too," Rick said. "When do I start and how much are you paying me?"

"The money is sweet, and you'll be living here, so you won't really have any expenses. How long do you need to make the move?"

"I can be back in the morning, ready to work."

"We'll talk actual figures later, but I'm sure you'll be satisfied with the accommodations and the wage," Gareth said. "See you for breakfast tomorrow?"

"You got it," Rick said as he left.

"That didn't last nearly long enough," Gareth said to the dripping Epiphano. "Let's go a couple of rounds, Pete. I'm in the mood to do a little sparring."

Half an hour later, Gareth walked into Billy's bedroom. He was sweating and a small cut on his brow bone trickled blood down his left temple. Tearing off his shirt, he used it to mop his armpits before throwing it on the floor. The bathroom door opened, and a naked Billy glared at the intruder.

"I'm busy. Get the hell out of here!"

Gareth's smile would have made a crocodile nervous. "Not until I get what I came for, you beautiful brat," he said.

"Get out of my room!" Billy shouted.

"I will," Gareth assured him as he dropped his trousers. "As soon as I've fucked you silly. I might even take the time to fuck you back to your senses."

"I'm not in the mood right now." Billy looked defiantly into the eyes of the man stalking purposefully toward him. "If you touch me, I'll kill you; I swear it."

"Keep it up, baby; you know I like it when you talk tough," Gareth said.

"Then you're really going to love this," Billy said.

Gareth ducked the punch the young man aimed at his head and wrapped his arms around Billy's supple frame. Billy writhed like a demon in a pentagram, but the big man held him fast. Pivoting to the right, Gareth pitched them both onto the bed.

"Fuck you, you bastard," Billy said, bucking under the other man's weight.

Gareth chuckled as he gathered Billy's wrists in one large hand. "Make me work for it, my darling devil."

"Get off me, arsehole!" Billy barked as Carey settled against him.

Gareth pinned one of the young man's thighs to the mattress with his knee and yanked the other leg over his shoulder. "You're so fucking beautiful," Gareth growled as he gazed down at Billy's manicured crotch.

"Fuck you," Billy replied.

Gareth nodded as though the young man had agreed with him. With his free hand, he gave his hard cock some finishing touches.

"Don't," Billy said as the blunt head touched his opening. "I swear I'll make you pay if you do this, Gareth."

Carey shivered and eased forward. The tip of his cock pushed through the opening and slid a few inches into the well-lubricated passage. "Good lad," he muttered absently in approval.

"Fucking bastard," Billy groaned.

Gareth moved his hips, working his shaft deeper in small increments.

"Damn you, you son of a bitch! Stop torturing me. Get it over with."

Gareth thrust, sheathing his length to the hilt, as he stared down into Billy's furious gaze. "There's no one else quite like you, tiger kitten," he said. "I hope you don't make me do something fatal to you some day. I'd miss you something rotten."

"Just fuck me if you're going to, you great ugly brute. You're killing the mood with all this chat."

Gareth was hard as granite and felt as though he could cum without moving another centimeter. This fractious lad excited him to a degree he'd not known was possible. No girl or woman, saint or whore, or any of the rent-boys or cellmates he'd played his rough games with, could compare with this insolent, devil may care live wire. Gareth enjoyed the role-playing precisely because he knew Billy wasn't afraid of him, not even a little.

With no further prelude, Gareth began to thrust, releasing Billy's hands to take up the young man's lolling cock. Billy squirmed restlessly, punching and pushing at Gareth's darkly pelted pectorals as he tried to unseat him. Gareth laughed giddily as he increased the speed and force of his stroke, leaning over Billy to look into the other man's eyes.

"You...bloody...bas...tard," Billy panted as Gareth pounded into him.

"Cum for me, baby," Gareth panted.

Billy blinked at this command as though waking from a trance and a convulsive shudder ran the length of his frame. Gareth groaned deeply as the tight sheath clamped down on his plunging cock. Clutching Billy's hip with bruising pressure, he worked the young man's limp shaft with his other hand.

"Fuh-uh-uh-uck...you," Billy stuttered with the force of Gareth's thrusts. "I ha-hate you, you fuh-fucker."

"Oh, hell yes, baby!" Gareth cried hoarsely as he buried his hard shaft in the clenching channel.

Billy squeezed his eyes shut as the big cock pulsed deep inside him. He imagined he could feel the bastard's seed flowing like venom into his system, becoming part of him, tainting him with the same evil. Despite these distressing thoughts, his smooth face wore a blank expression as his employer sank down to rest against his chest.

"That was absolutely marvelous," Gareth murmured, nipping lightly at Billy's neck. "You were bucking so hard that I thought you were going to throw us onto the floor a couple of times."

"Piss off."

"The game's over, dolly boy. You're not still sore, are you?"

"In quite a few places," Billy said. "Mind getting off me now?"

Gareth shifted his hips and pulled his wilting shaft free. Rolling onto his side, he scrubbed at his crotch with the top sheet. "You didn't cum," he said. "Again. If this continues, I'm going to start taking it personally, crumpet."

"You had more foreplay than I did," Billy said, flicking at the dried blood on the side of Gareth's face.

"Are you going shopping soon?" Gareth asked in a seeming non sequitur.

Billy gave the man a look that plainly asked if he were insane.

"Silly question," Gareth acknowledged. "While you're out spending my money, make sure you buy yourself a dildo, whatever type you fancy, and the next time I tell you to be ready for me, I want you to be ready."

"Whatever you want," Billy said and changed the subject. "Did you hire that nervy bloke from the bar?"

"Yes, I did. He made Epiphano look like a bumbling fool."

"I told you so."

"Yes, you did, you clever sausage," Gareth said. "I'm very glad I asked Barrow to send someone over to keep me company. Shame he got nicked, but his misfortune is my good luck since I get to keep you."

"You know something, Gareth? I think you hired Rick just so you can watch him insult me."

"Now why would I do that?"

"Because you revel in conflict and violence, you walking vat of testosterone."

"Oh yes, that's right," Gareth smirked as he sat up and began pulling on his trousers. "Listen, I have to meet with some blokes; business, you understand. I have to be there in person, but afterward, I could come back here and we could have a late dinner. How does that sound?"

"Boring," Billy said immediately. "Tell me where to meet you, and we'll party like lemmings."

Gareth was silent for a long moment as he bent to retrieve his discarded shirt.

"Fine. I don't want to go to your silly meeting, but is there a club nearby? I could wear something crotchless and you could fuck me right on the dance floor if it's crowded enough."

"Jesusmaryandjoseph," Gareth breathed. "Meet me at that Greek place you like."

"Acropolis Now?"

"Yeah, that one," Gareth leaned over the bed and grabbed a fistful of the young man's thick dark hair. "You don't know what you do to me when you say those nasty things with those pretty lips."

Billy surrendered his mouth as Gareth took bold possession. Drawing back, the crime boss looked down into his paramour's eyes.

"Crotchless," Billy whispered, smiling impishly.

"Be there," Gareth said and left before he lost control of himself again. The day was coming when he would have to think long and hard about the amount of influence Billy had over him. He needed to focus on consolidating his base of power here in the Colonies and the gorgeous spitfire was proving a major distraction. Gareth mustn't lose sight of the fact that Billy was a convenience, an appliance, a gadget that relieved stress. Someday, Gareth was going to have to point out these facts in a way that the lad wouldn't forget. Not today, though, Gareth thought with a sense of relief that he refused to acknowledge. Taking his hand from the doorknob of Billy's room, Gareth moved on down the hall.

After the man's footsteps finally faded, Billy got up and took another long, scalding hot shower.

# ~ Chapter Three ~

"THERE'S Carey," Graciela said to her partner.

Rick rose up a little in the backseat. "The thugs with him are Pete Epiphano and Paul Macross. Guess it's a two-bodyguard minimum tonight."

Graciela smirked and put down the tiny camera. "Marcial's boys are a different breed than Carey's," she observed.

"There's diversity even in the Mauve Mafia," Rick said, making his partner smother a giggle.

"I'm just saying that Perez and Allende are hardly the size of Epiphano and Macross."

"They're no less dangerous," Rick said. "Coral snakes aren't half the size of diamondbacks, but they're twice as lethal."

"*Gracias*," Graciela said. "Thanks for the herpetology lesson. If I'm ever on *Jeopardy* and the category is venomous snakes, I'm all set."

"Shit!" Rick said, sliding down in the seat.

Graciela looked out the back window and saw two men getting out of a new Maserati Quattroporte four cars behind them. One was big and beefy with the coldest eyes she'd ever seen; the other was young, coltish, and staggeringly attractive. Instead of entering the club across the street, the pair walked into the alley beside it.

"That was Levere," she said. "Is the kid Carey's punk?"

"He calls himself Billy Red," Rick said. "No idea if that's his name or not, but I wouldn't bet on it. I'll get the full name for you tomorrow."

"You do that, *hombre,* and in a few hours, I'll have his life history for you."

"You never disappoint," Rick said. "Now if you'll excuse me…"

Graciela sighed. "I don't think you should go snooping around here, but I can't stop you either."

Rick rolled his eyes. "If anyone spots me, I can always say that I was out looking for love in all the wrong places," he said. "Coincidences happen, you know."

"Just see that one doesn't happen to you," she said as he got out of the car.

"Okay, Mom. We already saw who Carey's meeting with. I'm just going to look down the alley and come right back, and then we can go, okay?"

Nonchalantly, Rick walked past the mouth of the alley and nearly stopped dead in his tracks, unable to believe what he was seeing. In the minimal shelter offered by a doorway, Levere was leaning against the

25

jamb with Billy at his feet. Billy was in the act of unzipping Levere's trousers. Mesmerized by the sheer audacity, Rick watched the young man pull the bodyguard's hard cock out through his fly. With a grace that ill befitted the alleyway setting, Billy leaned in and rubbed his cheek against the firm column of flesh. Levere's expression revealed his pleasure as the boss's private stock put out his tongue and lapped at the head of his arousal. The heavyset thug wrapped his big hands around his benefactor's skull and pushed the tip of his cock between the tempting lips. Billy didn't protest as Levere held his head in place and began thrusting into his mouth. The young man braced a hand against the brick wall and wrapped the other around the base of Levere's dick. Levere groaned deep in his chest and the small sound broke Rick's paralysis. The cop shook his head as he retraced his steps. He'd assessed Billy as reckless, but giving Levere head in public went far beyond mere flirting with disaster. The kid must have a death wish.

Graciela looked at Rick inquiringly when he got back in the car. "Nothing," Rick said. "Just a little dishonor among thieves."

"You're kidding," she said. "Levere and Carey's squeeze are getting it on in the alley? Man, that kid is hot stuff."

"He's a fool," Rick said. "A child who thinks he can go into the lion cage and pet the big kitties without getting hurt."

Graciela gave her partner a sidelong glance and continued the drive in silence. When they reached Rick's apartment building, she pulled over to the curb.

"*Buenos noches, guapo,*" she said warmly.

"Good night," Rick said, as he opened the door.

Graciela stuck her head out the window as he walked by. "Hey, Rick. One more thing before I go."

"Yeah?"

"We just saw Roger Levere escort Gareth Carey's toy boy to a club in a new Maserati. Carey arrived in a gorgeous BMW 760Li, and we know Antonio Marcial drives the biggest, plushest, whitest car that Cadillac makes. You and me are on a stakeout in a crappy old Chevy that smells like farts. Why is that?"

"I guess crime does pay, after all," Rick said. "Go get some downtime, *chica*. I'll call you when I get up tomorrow."

"You better. Good night, *mi hermano*."

WHEN Rick arrived for work, Gareth and Levere stood under the porte-cochere of the big house, about to get into the gleaming BMW sedan idling in the drive.

"We have to go out for a bit," Gareth said. "I'm going to trust you with one of my most treasured possessions. Billy wants to go shopping and I'd like you to escort him. Paul can tell you how we do things around here."

With that, Gareth got into the back and Levere got in after him. Epiphano glared at Rick from behind the wheel until Rick blew a kiss at him. Dropping the big car into gear, Epiphano drove away a bit faster than necessary.

Paul Macross was in the foyer and quick to draw down on Rick until he recognized him. "Sorry, man," Paul said. "I knew you were coming, but I get a little overzealous. Gareth left orders; you ready for a day on Rodeo Drive?"

Rick shrugged. "If that's what Gareth wants."

"It's what Billy wants," Paul said. "Which is almost the same thing these days."

Rick lowered his voice. "Are you telling me that Gareth is penis-whipped?" he asked.

Paul grinned. "Something like that. It'll pass. Meanwhile, you get to babysit."

"So, is he ready, or do I just wait around?"

Paul grinned again. "It's only ten o'clock. You've got a little while to wait. In the meantime, I'll show you where you'll be bunking. You'll like your new crib. The boss might be a stone-cold bastard that would kill you for looking at him cross-eyed, but he does take care of the help in style."

Rick picked up his bag and followed Paul to a nice set of rooms on the second floor where he was left alone to put his things away. When he was finished, he came down the stairs of the west wing and found Billy bitching out Paul in the front hall. The bodyguard saw Rick and an expression of relief spread over his face.

"Here's Rick now," Paul said. "I told you it would only be five minutes."

"And you were right," Billy said. "I'm sure this represents some sort of achievement for your species, but pardon me if I don't open any champagne. Shoo now." The young man waved Paul off. "You can go about your business."

"My pleasure," Paul said, shooting Rick a sympathetic look as he turned away.

"Are you ready?" Rick asked, sweeping past before Billy could speak.

The young man had no choice but to follow Rick outside if he wanted to talk to him. "Where are you going?" Billy called out.

"The garage. Unless you want to take my car."

"We didn't have to come outside to get to the garage," Billy pointed out.

"I like being outside," Rick said. "It's not all about you, you know."

"It is as long as you work for Gareth," Billy said as they walked into the enormous garage.

"No job is worth compromising my values," Rick said, looking around at the vehicles.

"Fuck, I just knew you were going to say something like that," Billy muttered.

"What?" Rick turned from admiring the silver Maserati Spyder.

"Nothing," Billy said. "You want to take that one?"

"Can we?"

Billy shrugged. "If the keys are in it, I don't think anyone can stop us."

"You wouldn't try to get me in trouble with the boss on first day, now would you?"

"I'm the one that put in a good word for you."

"True. Okay, you talked me into it. We'll take the Spyder."

A few breathless minutes later, Rick screeched to a stop behind a car pulling away from the curb and nabbed the parking space. As he turned off the powerful engine, he was aware of Billy staring at him over his sunglasses. "Abduction-evasion driving course," Rick said in answer to the inquiring look.

"Good job," Billy answered. "I think we lost all imaginary pursuit. Along with my breakfast."

"Bullshit. I know an adrenaline junkie when I see one," Rick said as he opened the door. "You loved it."

"Yeah," Billy dimpled in an inordinately appealing expression. "I did."

"Well, come on," Rick said brusquely. "Let's shop."

"Let me get one thing out of the way, and I can spend Gareth's money without worrying about it. You don't have to come into the shop if you don't want to."

"Very funny," Rick said. "Like I'd let you out of my sight. What the hell does a store called Shonen AImage sell, anyway?"

Billy opened the mirrored door and Rick followed him into the cool interior. It was immediately apparent to Rick why they didn't have their wares in the window. The shop obviously catered to an upscale, arty segment of the S&M and bondage crowd. The white walls were screens for projected images of anime-style characters in various compromising positions. The black shelves held dildos and other gadgets that looked like they came from C-3PO's toy chest.

Hanging from the ceiling were mannequins posed like superheroes of discipline, wearing the store's line of dominant/submissive gear. Rick was no prude, but a few of the items made him blink.

"Sure you don't want to wait outside?" Billy asked as a young Asian woman approached on five-inch stiletto heels of bright red patent leather.

"I'm fine," Rick said. "Take your time."

The undercover cop made a circuit of the store and arrived back at the counter as the sales clerk handed Billy a realistic-looking dildo. Hefting the flesh-colored false cock, Billy wrapped his fingers around it and shook his head. The leather cheongsam-clad woman said something in Japanese, and to Rick's surprise, Billy answered in the same language. Another dildo was taken from the glass case and presented with a small bow. Obviously produced by the same manufacturer, this phallus differed from the last only in length and circumference as evidenced by Billy's failure to get his fist around it. A few more soft words in Japanese and the toy was carefully wrapped in black tissue paper and placed in a silver box tied with crimson ribbon. It then went into an elegant black and silver bag with the shop's name dripping redly down the side.

"Let's go," Billy said. "I feel the need to spend more of Gareth's money than usual today."

Rick didn't comment as he followed the kid in and out of stores as Billy tried on and purchased enough clothing, shoes, and accessories for a long cruise. Three hours and somewhere around eleven thousand dollars later, Billy asked if Rick was hungry. To Rick's surprise, the young man didn't lead them to a trendy expensive bistro, but to a Lebanese man with a cart. Billy asked for a vegetarian kebab and Rick told the man to make it two. Adding bottles of water to their purchases, they carried the food back to the car. At the first bite, they realized just how hungry they were and devoured the wraps. Rick forgot for a moment that they weren't just two ordinary human beings fulfilling a basic need. He grinned at Billy as he displayed his empty wrapper, licked clean of spicy hummus smears.

"Man, I really wolfed that down," he said.

"Mmm," Billy said, licking tahini from his fingers. "That was good. Don't you love it when the tabbouleh is freshly made and…" The young man words trailed off as he looked up at Rick's silhouette haloed by the late afternoon sun. Without his shades, Billy's eyes were dazzled as the light turned the ends of Rick's hair into a golden corona, masking his strong features with shadow. For that moment, he could have been any big, blond man, and Billy felt a pang of longing so powerful he almost doubled over.

"You okay?" Rick asked. "You look like you saw a ghost."

"Sorry. Why am I bothering you with my chatter? You probably want to get back and polish your bullets, or whatever you hard cunts do when you're not shooting people."

Rick raised his eyebrows. "You taking anything for those mood swings?" he asked.

"Just drive me home, please," Billy said, crumpling his wrapper and tossing it to the floor of the sports car.

Rick reached across and picked up the ball of paper, placing it in the bag with his. "Home it is," he said equably.

Rick parked the Spyder in the garage and Billy got out immediately. As the kid hurried away, Rick made a snap decision to speak about the thing he'd been mulling over all day. "Hang on a second." Rick got out and faced Billy across the hood. "You're going to tell me, quite rightly, that this is none of my business, but I have to say it. Not necessarily because I care about you, or have a heart of gold, but because I'll probably get stuck disposing of your carcass when Gareth catches you screwing around."

"What the fuck are you talking about?"

"I was in several dressing rooms with you today," Rick said. "I saw the bruises. Hey, maybe I'm just naïve and you like it that way, but I don't think you do. And if you keep playing with fire…well, you know what they say."

"What the bloody fuck are you talking about?"

"I'm referring to your clandestine activities with Levere, or does Gareth know about that?"

"I doubt it," Billy said.

"Well, what do you think he'd do if he found out?"

"I'm not sure, but I'll bet it's the same thing he'd do if he found out you were a cop."

Rick stared at the young man, hoping his shock didn't show on his face. "Why would you say something like that? Are you trying to get me killed?"

"Relax," Billy said. "I'm not going to tell anybody."

"There's nothing to tell," Rick said, coming around the car.

Billy leaned close to Rick and spoke softly. "Is that right, Officer Miles?"

Rick's blood ran cold as fjord water, as his brain went into overdrive trying to figure out how Billy knew his name.

"You didn't nick me for anything," Billy said. "I saw you when you visited London a few years ago. You attended a ceremony in which officers from police forces around the world were honored."

"I was part of an honor guard," Rick remembered. "Of course, that was before I came out of the closet. Not many honors after that."

Billy nodded his understanding of all that Rick's words implied. "You didn't quit though," he said.

Rick hesitated before he spoke again. "We can talk about it sometime, if you want, but not here."

"Do we have an understanding then?"

Rick mimed zipping his lips and reached into the car for the shockingly small number of bags that represented so much money spent.

"Hey, one more thing. I was wondering; why does Gareth call you all those weird pet names?" Rick asked, as Billy took the bags off his hands at the stairs.

"Who knows?" Billy looked back over his shoulder and shrugged as he started up the steps. "He's mad," the young man said simply. "A genuine lunatic."

Rick frowned and went to the office Paul had shown him. Gareth was there, talking on the phone behind a massive mahogany desk. Epiphano sat in a comfortable chair flipping through a magazine. The big man looked up at Rick and scowled before returning to his reading.

"Rick," Gareth said as he hung up. "How was your day?"

"Uneventful," Rick said. "And yours?"

"Afraid I can't say the same, mate," Gareth answered. "I had a very exciting meeting today with a new vendor. This supplier is currently overstocked and willing to part with product for a greatly reduced price so long as we buy in bulk. Naturally, this means that the deal with the Mexican Mafia is off. I just can't come up with that much cash."

Rick pursed his lips. "High-Tone won't be happy if you break the deal."

"The deal's broken," Gareth said, leaning forward in his chair. "All except for telling Marcial about it. I need you to do that for me, Rick."

"Do I look suicidal?" Rick asked.

"That's the task I'm setting you," Gareth said. "Smooth this over with High-Tone, or make the problem go away however you see fit. Your reward will match the deed."

"This is the real test, isn't it?" Rick said.

"It will certainly prove your worth," Gareth replied. "Do you think I'd even consider sending Epiphano or Levere?"

Movement drew Rick's gaze to the window behind Gareth. Billy had changed into a Speedo and was walking out to the pool. The bright red bathing suit demanded attention, but Rick dragged his eyes back to his boss. "When?" Rick asked.

"That's entirely up to you," Gareth said. "But the sooner the better."

Rick looked out the window again at the blue sky, white clouds, and tanned body in red Lycra, and smiled. "It's a good day to die," he said.

"I like your spirit. Come and find me when you get back."

"Will do," Rick said as he left the room.

For about two seconds, standing there in the hall, Rick considered walking out the door and walking away from the case. Hell, it wasn't even an official case and one of the gang had already seen through his cover. He had no guarantee Billy wouldn't inform on him as soon as he was gone and now he had the wild card of a new set of drug dealers. It was starting to fall apart fast. He should cut his losses before he lost everything.

The two seconds passed and Rick continued down the hall and out to his car. He had a good idea where High-Tone Marcial could be found at this time of day.

# ~ Chapter Four ~

*"HOLA, carnale!"*

Rick grinned at the greeting and embraced the man that delivered it, answering in kind. *"Muy bonito!"* Rick exclaimed as he squeezed Marcial's ass cheek.

The handsome Latin man smiled warmly and gestured to a chair. "Sit, *mi vero amigo,* and tell me what you want now."

"I know I'm a big pain in your excellent ass right now, but I need another favor."

"And what might that be?" Marcial asked, dismissing Perez and Allende with his eyes.

"Don't kill me right away."

"Why should I want to kill you?"

"I'm here to tell you that Mr. Carey is backing out of your deal."

Marcial rose to his feet and glared at the undercover cop. *"Que barbaridad!"* High-Tone shouted. *"Mierda, pendejo. Un vero cabron. Ai!"* The door opened and Allende stuck his head in only to be angrily ordered back out. Marcial took several deep breaths and sat back down. "What is that asshole thinking?"

"He says he found another vendor that'll undercut your price."

*"Chingate!"* Marcial swore hotly. "Who would be so…*pendejada*! I can't believe it!"

"I told him," Rick said. "I told him you'd be pissed, but he…"

"He already thinks he runs El Lay," Marcial finished for him.

"Something like that," Rick nodded. "He has no fear, Tonio. I'll admit this to you and my partner and no one else, but Hairy Carey scares me."

"Then do something about this *chi-chi cabron*," Marcial said. "Or you can bet your boots that I will."

Rick smiled again. "You still say 'bet your boots.'"

"And you still look like the shit-kicker you really are, *caballero*," Marcial said.

"Kicked your ass a few times, if that's what you mean," Rick answered.

"Hey, cowboy," Marcial said, abruptly serious. "I owe you a debt that is impossible to repay. What is a sister's life worth, eh? If not for you, Penelope would not have lived to marry and give me nieces and nephews to spoil."

"But?"

Marcial cast his eyes toward the ceiling, took a deep breath, and faced Rick again. "It shames me to have to say these words. I understand that you want to arrest this *cabron* and regain your good reputation, but I am afraid that will not happen. My instincts tell me that this Englishman will die soon."

"Tonio, don't," Rick said. "Don't start a war because a tourist was rude to you. Let me take him down. I need this collar."

"There are many high-profile criminals in this town," Marcial said. "Pick another one."

"I can't start over, Tonio," Rick said. "I'm in with Carey, and I'm staying. If you come after him, you'll find me standing guard. I know it's fucked up, but that's the way it is."

The two men locked eyes for a long moment before the opening of the door broke the tension. Marcial's dark eyes glinted with suppressed anger as he turned.

"Sorry," Perez said. "Mrs. Fortunato's on the phone. You're gonna be late, *patron*."

Marcial nodded curtly. "Tell her I'm on my way," he said. "Rick…. *Ai, Dios mio*, this is not right. I don't want you to get hurt, but I can't let this *picaflor* disrespect me."

Rick stood. "You've got someplace to be," he said. "And I've delivered my message. I'll get going now."

"Birthday party," Marcial said. "Eight years ago today, my nephew Fernando came into the world."

"Congratulate Penelope for me," Rick said. "She's the one that did all the work."

Marcial chuckled and stood to embrace Rick warmly. *"Vaya con Dios,"* he said.

"Promise me you'll think about backing off," Rick said.

Marcial opened the door for the policeman. "Sure," he said. "And you think about getting the hell away from that *Diablo loco*. If not me, someone will come after him. He pushes too hard, too fast. Nobody wants to do business with a madman."


"YOU'RE still in one piece," Epiphano greeted Rick.

"You sound disappointed," Rick observed.

Epiphano shrugged. "I'm cooled off, mate," he said. "You were just trying to impress the boss, and I won't hold a grudge against you for that."

"Good," Rick said. "I like a nice, cordial working atmosphere."

Epiphano almost smiled. "Come on," the muscleman said. "Gareth will want to talk to you."

"There you are," Gareth said brightly as Rick entered his office. "Somehow I knew you were going to come back. Geordie, this is Rick that I was telling you about."

Rick turned as a big man with several days' worth of dark stubble stood and extended a hand. Rick returned Geordie's firm grip and turned to Gareth. "Any relation?" Rick asked, looking from Gareth to Geordie and back.

Gareth shook his head. "A lot of people ask that, but no, we're not related. Geordie worked for me back in the UK. He managed to find his way back to my side despite the best efforts of police on two continents to keep us apart."

Gareth and Geordie's eyes met with a click that was almost audible. Rick raised an eyebrow, as the tension grew tauter with each passing moment. The undercover cop resisted the mad urge to scream at them to go ahead and fuck, or fight, or both.

"Bloody hell," Billy said from the doorway. "Where did you come from? You're as handsome as Gareth and just as big."

"Bigger where it counts," Geordie smirked. "What's this then? Up to your old games, Gareth lad?"

"Billy, this is Geordie Cook," Gareth said. "He was my head of security back home. Geordie, this tasty wee bit of crumpet goes by Billy Red."

"Too right he does," Geordie laughed. "I've seen you before, love. In London."

Billy struck a pose of polite interest. "I'm afraid I don't recall."

"It'll come to you," Geordie said. "I'm a little tired from the trip, Gareth. Mind if I bow out?"

Gareth shook his head. "I need to talk to Rick anyway. Billy, would you show Geordie to a room? Pete, stay for a minute." After the door had closed again, Gareth gestured to Rick to speak.

"Marcial took it like I said he would: like a cattle prod where the sun don't shine. He threatened to kill you, which I would take seriously."

"Damned right I take it seriously," Gareth said, getting to his feet. "If Marcial says he's going to kill me, I expect him to try. I knew that when I made the new deal and I told all of my employees that security would have to be even tighter from now on. Isn't that right, Pete?" Gareth asked.

"You sure did, Gareth," Epiphano answered.

"Are you working for Marcial, Pete?"

"What?" Epiphano looked confused.

"Rick," Gareth said, turning his laptop around on his desk. "Come here; I want you to see something. You, too, Pete; come on around the desk. Okay, what are we looking at here?" Gareth said, tapping the screen with a laser pointer.

"It's the feed from the camera in the foyer," Epiphano said immediately.

"That's right," Gareth said. "This footage is from a couple of hours ago, when you, Pete, were on duty." The three men watched as the door opened and a young man came in carrying three pizza boxes. He set them on the foyer table, picked up the money lying there, and left.

"You can see he didn't do anything," Epiphano said quickly. "I was watching him on the monitor the whole time."

"He was in the house alone," Gareth said sharply. "He could have left a bomb!" On the last word, Gareth drove the stainless-steel pointer into Epiphano's hand, pinning it to the desk. Epiphano cried out, but had the presence of mind to keep his hand still instead of jerking it away and doing even more damage. Rick gritted his teeth, leaned forward, and yanked the pen from the man's hand.

"What the bloody fuck compelled you to do that?" Gareth asked coldly.

"Because it's stupid to maim a man that you're counting on to protect you," Rick said, his heart hammering. "And you're not stupid, Gareth."

"Pete," Gareth said without turning around. "Go and get your hand looked at. And, Pete? If you fail me again, I'll nail something else of yours to my desk." Epiphano didn't speak as he left. Gareth held out his hand to Rick and after a moment, Rick gave the drug dealer his pointer back. As he did so, Rick readied himself to defend against an attack, but Gareth simply put the implement on the desk. The gang leader's rage appeared to have dissipated as quickly as it had flared.

"Thanks," Gareth said. "I lost my temper. Nothing personal."

"I know that, Gareth, and my job is to look out for you, and that's what I'm going to do."

"You'll even protect me from myself?"

"If you let me," Rick said. "So is Geordie going to be in charge now?"

Gareth nodded. "He's good at what he does. A hard man, but that's what the job needs."

"Hard, huh," Rick said drolly. "You mean compared to softies like you?"

Gareth smiled. "I hope I never find myself at odds with him. Are you hungry, thirsty, horny? Need anything?"

"I'm good," Rick said. "I think I'll head off to bed."

"Good night then and good job, Rick, all around."

Rick walked through the big house to the west wing as the adrenaline drained from his system, marveling at the fact that he was still alive. He entered the hall that led to his quarters and saw that the door of the room across from his was open. As he drew closer, he could hear Geordie's voice.

"Billy Rose. Still as pretty as your name. Remember me now?" the man asked.

"Unfortunately," Billy replied calmly. "That hurts, by the way."

"I was pretty sure it did," Geordie said. "Pain is the only reliable way to get a whore's full attention. Now I can be sure you're hearing me. What are you doing here?"

"What does it look like?"

"It looks like you're spreading your legs for the boss."

"So what? I'm not allowed to better myself?"

"Sure you are," Geordie said. "The question before us is: Does Gareth know about your past, and if he did, would he care?"

"No," Billy said. "The question before us is: What will I do to make sure you keep your mouth shut?"

"You're really pretty when you're pissed off," Geordie said. "How about a down payment?"

"Go ahead and tell Gareth. He knows I worked for Mr. Barrow."

"And before that?" Geordie asked silkily. "Would you really want me to tell him about your misspent youth?"

"Let go of me."

"Why so unfriendly? Pretend I'm the boss and take some dick-tation."

"That's a horrid pun and you look a right wanker grabbing yourself like that," Billy said. "Do you intend to keep me here by force?"

"I won't have to. You're a smart lad. You know as well as I do that Gareth will look at you differently if I tell him you were a footpath-walking rent-boy who ended up in the nick. He's careful where he sticks his willy, Gareth is."

There was a long enough silence to make Rick wonder what was going on and then Geordie made a yummy noise. "Mmm-hmmmmm, that's better," Geordie purred. "Personally, I like a lover with experience, but a lot of guys are hung up on that virgin/slut thing. I think we both know what kind of guy Gareth is. Yeah, that's nice. Get me good and hard, and I'll shag you against the wall."

Rick put a hand on the door and called out, "Hello, neighbor," as he swung it open.

Geordie's head snapped toward Rick, quickly assessing the degree of threat he posed. "Mate," he said. "Is your timing always this bad?"

Billy yanked his hand from Geordie's pants when the door opened, and now stood looking everywhere but at Rick.

"I couldn't have interrupted anything very private," Rick said. "Unless this is Billy's twin."

Geordie leaned closer to Rick. "Gareth says you come highly recommended, so I assume you know how to be discreet. Keep your gob shut about this."

"I get the picture," Rick said. "Gareth gave me the chain of command. It goes from you to Gareth, to God. Did I get the order right?"

"Gareth also told me you were cheeky," Geordie said. "I don't mind cheek as long as there's respect at the back of it. What I don't like are people who enter without knocking."

"And people that don't want company shouldn't leave the door open," Rick said. "I did call out, which I didn't really want to do. If you had been unfriendlies, I would have completely lost the advantage of surprise."

Geordie's scowl eased. "True," he said. "You have a suspicious nature, Rick. I like that in a bloke."

"Thanks. I'm off to bed, unless you have any instructions for me."

"I'll come with you," Billy said. "I need to show you which items to return to the store."

"I'll see you later, then," Geordie said as Billy and Rick left.

"Thanks," Billy said to Rick when the door closed behind them.

"I'm the protector of lost boys," Rick said. "I told you that when we met."

"I remember," Billy said, looking to his left. "Your suite's down there, right?"

Rick nodded. "Yeah. It's really nice," he said neutrally, wondering what point Billy was coming to.

"Could we talk?" the young man asked.

Rick roused himself from the exhaustion of post-adrenaline rush. "Sure," he said and led the way to his quarters. "I've had a hard day," Rick said as he shut the door. "So let's be as brief as possible."

"Hard?" Billy said. "Someday I'll have to get your definition of hard. Right now, I'd like your assurance you won't mention anything to Gareth about what you just saw."

"That's your business," Rick said.

"I wasn't conducting business," Billy said sharply.

"Well, one of you was," Rick answered. "Sounded like bartering to me."

A veil dropped over Billy's eyes. "As you said, it hardly concerns you."

"Unless it affects my ability to do my job," Rick said. "I was hired to keep Mr. Carey from getting hurt, which I had to remind him of a little while ago."

"I see. You're going to keep me from breaking his heart, are you? Don't waste your time; he hasn't got one."

"Then why are you with him?" Rick asked bluntly.

Billy rubbed his thumb over his fingertips in the universal sign for cash.

"Money?" Rick said. "Bullshit. You're beautiful and sexy as hell; you could have your pick of wealthy men."

"More like wealthy men have had their pick of me," Billy said.

"Don't expect violins," Rick said. "Everybody has it tough."

Billy nodded. "Thanks for reminding me. I guess you'd like me to leave."

Rick's heart twisted in his chest. It could hear Billy's unspoken plea. It wanted Rick to tell Billy to stay. It wanted Rick to comfort Billy. "I'm really beat," Rick made himself say. "I'm sure we'll see each other tomorrow and we can talk more, if you want."

"Yeah," Billy said. "I still want to hear about your coming out. I'm always at the pool until lunchtime."

After the young man left, Rick flopped on his bed and lay there on his back with his feet on the floor. He stared up at the high ceiling and willed his thoughts to cease their flight. He didn't like the direction they were taking. Rick told himself he could not go soft now. He absolutely could not feel sorry for the brittle, jaded toy boy. Under no circumstances must he start to care about Billy. Billy Rose, if he had heard Geordie right. What Rick needed to do was pass Billy's full name on to Graciela. With a concrete short-term goal decided upon, Rick's racing mind finally took a break. And that's when Billy tiptoed into his thoughts like a cat burglar. Billy was what he was, but there was no denying that the kid was a smokin' hot piece of ass.

As Rick relaxed, his mind drifted drowsily until it settled on the image of Billy as he'd looked the first day Rick had come to the house: Billy by the pool, dripping wet, skin gleaming in the sun, his wet white thong nearly transparent, clearly showing the curve of his long cock. In Rick's dozy fantasy, Billy bent over and pulled aside the string that ran up his butt crack. Rick's hand wrapped more firmly around his stiffening length, as limber Billy touched his toes and gave Rick an inviting look from between his legs. The undercover cop squeezed his cock, picturing the tip entering the kid's glistening hole. Closing his eyes as his breathing grew labored, Rick shuttled his fist up and down his hard shaft, imagining Billy's moans and soft cries as he thrust into him.

"Oh yeah, Rick, that feels so good," Billy purred as he rocked back against the man that rode him. "You're making me cum."

"Cum for me," Rick murmured and fantasy-Billy spurted a milky stream into the pool.

Moving more quickly now, Rick shunted his aching length in the clinging sheath. Billy ground back against his pelvis, rolling his hips as he flexed his thighs, bearing down on Rick's shaft as it pistoned in and out. Rick leaned over Billy's back, nuzzling the damp skin as his climax broke open, spilling hot jolts of bliss that ran together in one electrifying moment of ecstasy. Still holding his spent rod, Rick dropped into dreams with cum drying on his belly.

# ~ Chapter Five ~

RICK woke early, as usual, and went to the exercise room. Geordie was there already with Levere as spotter, and Rick lifted an eyebrow at the weight the man was pressing. Waiting until Geordie replaced the barbell on the rack, Rick commented. "Impressive."

Do you lift?" Geordie asked as he sat up.

Rick shook his head as he found a clear space and began his warm-up breathing and stretching. Geordie exchanged a glance with Levere.

"What're you getting ready for, mate?" Levere asked. "Swan-fucking-Lake?"

"Nope, just some yoga to loosen me up before the tai chi."

"I hear you really showed Pete up," Geordie said. "Gareth says you can handle yourself. That says a lot coming from him. He's not easily impressed."

Rick snorted. "I've noticed. He's got the buffest bodyguards, the coolest cars, the stateliest mansion and the hottest…. Help me out here. How do you refer to Billy?"

"A pain in the ass," Levere said instantly. "But he's no bimbo. I wish he was, but that lad is shrewd on a stick. He's clever at putting ideas into the boss's head. You watch; Billy will act like the new suppliers are beneath him, but he's the one who brought them to Gareth's attention in the first place."

"Don't you worry about young Mr. Rosie," Geordie said, watching his reflection flex in the wall of mirrors. "I've got his number. The day is coming when the sun will no longer shine from Billy's tight little arse."

Levere leered at Geordie. "I'd like to find out just how tight," he said.

"That's easy," Geordie said. "All you need is a million pounds, a ton of coke, and a dangerous look. I'm one out of three, but that's more than you."

Levere smirked like a man that knows more than his audience does. "You think I couldn't have Billy if I wanted him?"

"Oh, you want him," Geordie said confidently. "Every-fuckin-body wants Billy. Shit, even straight guys that meet him probably beat off to a fantasy of him blowing them. Am I right, Rick?"

Rick looked over. "Sorry; wasn't listening," he lied.

"Why ask Miller? He's gay," Levere put in, turning to Rick. "Right?"

"Unless you're interested in me, I don't see how that's any of your business," Rick said.

"Come on, mate," Geordie said. "We're just being guys here. Shootin' the shit, as you Yanks say."

"Well, if you must know," Rick said. "I try not to limit myself, and I don't like labels."

"Is that it?" Levere said.

Geordie chuckled. "Let me be more specific. Would you give young Willem Rosen a root?"

"Sure," Rick said. "If I had a bulletproof suit and a non-flammable dick."

Levere and Geordie both laughed. "I'm starting to see what Gareth likes about you," Geordie said.

"Another conquest," Rick said lightly, licking his finger and making a mark in the air. "So Billy's real name is Willem Rose?"

"Rosen," Geordie corrected. "Another edge I have over our Aussie friend. I knew Billy back in England. He was calling himself by his proper name the last I heard of him, but here he is, Billy Red again, bigger than life and just as fucked up."

"Was he a pro?" Rick asked as he stretched to reach a towel. Levere grabbed the towel and tossed it to Rick. Rick nodded his thanks as he mopped at his face and neck.

"A pro? You mean a prozzie?" Levere asked.

"What that lad doesn't know about pleasing a man isn't worth knowing," Geordie said. "Does that answer your question, Rick?"

"Not really," Rick said. "I'm just curious about the people I live with, but if this is a sensitive subject for you…"

"Easy, sport," Geordie said. "Let's not start pissing on each other just yet."

Rick gave the Brit an easy smile. "It was just a little snap o' the towel, bro," he said. "It didn't mean anything."

Mollified, Geordie took a long swallow of his water. "Billy started on the streets when he was around fifteen. Ran with a gang of rent-boys that sort of looked out for one another. Then a fella by the name of Barrow recruited him. Barrow had a stable of the most beautiful boys and girls you ever saw. Underage, a lot of 'em, but it was better than the street or the nick. Barrow catered to the bosses of the drug trafficking network, supplying fresh flesh for parties and escort work."

"I get the picture," Rick said.

"That's when I met him," Geordie went on. "I was working for the late, unlamented Jerry Villiers. Jerry was everybody's mate until they found out he was gathering evidence for the police in order to keep his lily-white arse out of lockup. They found him on the steps of police headquarters with a Sicilian necktie."

"What the fuck is that?" Levere asked.

"It's a punishment the Mafia used to save for squealers," Rick said. "The throat is cut from ear to ear and the tongue pulled down through the gash."

"That's right," Geordie said. "Someone pulled the little canary's tongue right out."

"Strewth," Levere frowned. "That's harsh."

"He was an arsehole," Geordie said. "I met Billy because this arsehole procured him for the evening. Villiers was legless before the lad even arrived and pounced on him the second he cleared the door. Despite the tosser's drunken state, Billy was as accommodating as only a thousand-pound-a-night hooker can be."

"Does this story come to a point anytime soon?" Rick asked.

"Thought you were curious, mate," Geordie replied.

"Go on," Levere said. "I want to hear your story."

"As I was saying, there's Billy giving it his all, but Villiers' willy is limp as linguine. He's so drunk he can't get hard. Naturally, the arsehole decides that this is Billy's fault and that if he can't fuck Billy, he'll fuck Billy with the bottle of Scotch."

"Strike me pink!" Levere exclaimed. "The dirty little bastard. Did he do it?"

"I had to help him, but yeah, he did it," Geordie said. "And I'll be buggered if he didn't get hard after all."

"The things they expect us to do for a paycheck, huh?" Rick said sardonically.

Geordie met Rick's gaze. "Don't waste your time feeling bad for me, or Billy," Geordie said. "He was cool as ice cream. Even reminded me to put the cap on the bottle."

"That's simple self-preservation," Rick said. "I'll see you later."

"Rick's got a tender heart," Geordie said to Levere as Rick walked away.

"At least I've got one," Rick muttered.

Rick walked outside and down the terraced decks to the pool. Billy was doing laps while Epiphano sat under an umbrella reading a fitness magazine. Returning Epiphano's nod, Rick jogged down the path across the back lawn to the greenbelt of dogwood and blue spruce. As soon as he thought he was reasonably out of range of listening devices, he took out his cell phone and dialed Graciela's private number. "*Hola, chica,*" he said brightly, happy to be talking to a friend. "What's shakin'? I've got a name for you and some info on a new gang of suppliers. Who's the man?"

"Rick," Graciela said. "Hang on a minute, *hombre*. I have to tell you something."

"Damn right, you do. I need any and all information on…"

"Rick," Graciela interrupted. "Listen to me, *hermano*. Something happened last night."

"What?" Rick's ebullient mood evaporated.

"There was a bomb," she said. "At the home of Penelope Fortunato. She's…"

"Tell me what happened, Gracie," Rick interrupted.

"I'm trying. It was a goddamned drive-by bombing. There was a party…"

"A birthday party," Rick interrupted again. "Oh, God, is everyone all right?"

"No," Graciela said. "I'm sorry, Rick. Antonio Marcial was killed shielding his nephew from the blast. Marcial's bodyguards also perished as a result of… Shit, I sound like a goddamned newsbitch. I'm really sorry, *hermano*."

"What about Penelope? And the kids?"

"Hang on." Rick heard the sound of snuffling and the rustle of tissue. "Sorry. Penelope and her family are fine, but we don't really have anything to go on as far as who did this. Nobody got a look at the car or anyone in it. The family isn't talking to the press, as you can imagine. They're staying at an undisclosed location."

"Where?" Rick demanded.

"Don't," Graciela said. "Don't blow your cover over this. The bombing is being investigated and they don't need your help."

"I just want to see Penny and tell her…" Rick's words trailed off.

"Right," Graciela said. "What could you say to her right now? She's surrounded by cops and her family; she'll be fine. You just watch out for your fine ass."

"Why would I need to do that? You're watching it for me."

"That's better," Graciela said. "Put the bad news away for later."

"Sure," Rick said. "But I think I'm a lot closer to the perpetrator than anyone on the case."

"You sure? Carey's moving up fast, but would he challenge Marcial at this point?"

"He's not rational, Gracie," Rick said. "He may have sent me to see Tonio just to put him off guard. Who knows?"

"I know that I want Carey more than ever now," Graciela said. "I got a real hard-on for him."

"Good. Here's what I know. Carey backed out of his deal with Tonio for a better one. Seems there's a group of cowboys out there with a butt-load of blow they need to get rid of pronto. My guess is that they hijacked it."

"*Pendejos!* Who would be so *loco* to steal from drug traffickers?"

"I'll be finding out soon," Rick said. "Carey invited them here to seal the deal. They actually agreed. They're either bulletproof, or crazy, like you said."

"What about the boyfriend?"

"The boyfriend's got more than one alias, but his real name is Willem Rosen. Try the London cops for information on him, specifically Vice. I get the feeling this kid is not what he seems. For one thing, he tries to hide it, but he's a lot smarter than your average himbo. Hell, he could be running this outfit using Carey as a beard for all we know."

"Some things in life aren't what they seem," Graciela said. "Other things are exactly what they seem. Knowing the difference is what we call wisdom."

"Is that an old Spanish saying?"

"I have no idea. It was in some movie I saw. You sound better; you okay?"

"No Gracie, I'm nowhere near okay, but I'm glad I have someone that cares about me the way you do."

There was a moment of silence and then Graciela spoke, her voice curiously thicker. "It's my job," she said. "We're partners, you worthless cock-hound. Now don't do anything stupid like confronting Carey about the bomb. I'll have something for you when you call in again."

"Thanks, Gracie. Take care."

"Love you, *hombre*," Graciela said, but he had already hung up.

# ~ Chapter Six ~

RICK pocketed his phone and turned to walk back up the slope. As he reached the pool deck, he saw Billy toweling off near the deep end and a group gathered up by the bar. Gareth beckoned, but Billy stopped Rick as the undercover cop passed by him.

"Hi," the kid said. "Have a nice jog?"

"Yeah. It's pretty here," Rick said. "I'd love to chat, but the boss wants me."

"Doesn't everybody?" Billy smiled impishly.

Rick frowned slightly at the flirtatious note in the young man's voice. "I know you come on to other men to make Gareth jealous," he said. "But you're wasting it this time. He can't hear you."

"Then you'd better get a move on, hadn't you?" Billy's tone went chilly. "You wouldn't want to make him suspicious."

"Thanks for the reminder," Rick said as he walked away. As he approached the shaded tables around the bar, Rick cursed himself for not telling Gracie that Billy knew he was a cop. He had his reasons, but he knew it was a mistake that would probably come back to bite him on the ass.

"Rick!" Gareth called out. "Come and join us. Meet my new friends."

Rick was scoping the strangers as he walked toward them and he didn't have a good impression so far. The three men were in their early twenties, but they dressed even younger, closer to junior high. Their clothing was pure skate dawg and they had the bed-head look down to an art. Rick stopped trying to count the piercings and tattoos meant to convince the onlooker that these were very bad boys indeed.

"I hope I get your names right, gentlemen," Gareth said with exaggerated brightness. "Rick, meet Nathan Fine, Rafael Novacelli, and Flip; it is Flip, right? Flip Hudson, I love it. Together, they're the Kookie Kutter Krew, with three Ks." Carey chuckled.

Rick nodded in a cordial manner, wondering what Gareth was planning. Whatever it was, the boss obviously hadn't shared it with anyone else. Carey's light-hearted manner made Rick frankly nervous. Almost as nervous as the way Fine was looking at Rick as though trying to place a familiar face.

"Don't I know you?" Fine said.

"It's possible you've seen me. You watch *America's Most Wanted*?"

"Are you bustin' on me?" Fine asked with an edge to his voice.

"Rick does that," Gareth said. "I don't know why I suffer it. However, we're not here to talk about personnel; we're here to talk about product."

"That's our cue," Flip said.

"I'm not deaf," Fine said. "Sorry, Gareth. We're prepared to deliver the product, after you test it, at the amount and price discussed. However…"

Fine snapped his fingers and Novacelli tore his gaze from Billy's crotch to fumble in one of the many pockets of his baggy shorts. The morose-looking punk found what he sought and tossed it to Fine. Fine turned back to Gareth, and Novacelli's gaze swung immediately back to Billy. Rick moved to the other side of the bar, stopping beside the ever-vigilant Epiphano as he watched Gareth Carey discuss business with the new suppliers. Rick didn't know for certain that Gareth had ordered the bombing of Marcial's sister's house, but it was a better than fifty-fifty chance. The undercover cop couldn't fathom how anyone could blow up an eight-year-old child's birthday party and not show some sign of it.

"He's real pretty," Rafael Novacelli interrupted Rick's thoughts, as he came up to the bar.

Rick followed the direction of Novacelli's stare and wasn't surprised to see Billy. The young man had pulled on a pair of black track pants, but his sculpted upper torso was still bare as he walked toward the bar. Gareth hooked an arm around Billy's waist and reeled him in as he walked past. Billy pouted, accepted a kiss on the cheek, and turned to look over his shoulder at the bar. Novacelli thought Billy was looking at him and gazed back like an entranced cobra. Billy raised his hand as though curled around a glass and mimed tossing back a drink.

"You want to suck me?" Novacelli said in surprise, misunderstanding the hand signals completely.

Rick turned to look at the punk. "What did you say?"

Novacelli's stare didn't waver, nor did he answer. He didn't hear Rick's question. He was in his own world, a world where Billy was on his knees confessing his irresistible attraction and begging for just a taste of Novacelli's dick. "I would love it if you sucked me and I'd love to do something really nice for you too," Novacelli whispered.

"Hey," Rick snapped his fingers in the drug dealer's face. "Who the hell are you talking to, punk?"

Epiphano tapped Rick's shoulder and handed him a tall glass filled with ice and clear liquid. "Make yourself useful," Epiphano said. "Take Billy a drink."

"Keep an eye on that guy," Rick looked pointedly at Novacelli. "His wheel is spinning, but his hamster died a long time ago."

"I'm keeping both eyes on all of these snot-nosed wigger ratbags," Epiphano said. "I don't care how cheap their drugs are; these dickheads are no bargain."

Glad he wasn't the only one worried about the gang, Rick carried the drink to Billy. Gareth threw an arm around Rick's shoulders and turned him to face the dealers. "What do you think of the Kookies?" Gareth asked.

"Kutters," Flip said. "We call ourselves the Kutters."

"Of course you do," Gareth said equably. "Well, Rick?"

"These boys look like they could be a real handful," Rick said. "I'd have to see them work to have an opinion though."

"You better hope you never see us go to work," Fine said. "Most people don't survive the experience."

"Oooh," Rick shivered. "Real bad boys, aren't you? I'll try not to piss you off."

"You're smarter than you look," Fine said and then addressed Gareth. "You've really got the life, dog. Cushy pad, sweet ride, stone-cold soldiers, and this honey on your arm. I won't be shy; I'll flat out tell you what's what. I want what you have."

Rick felt Gareth's muscles tense and readied himself to act, but Gareth chuckled warmly.

"Of course you do," he said again. "But you don't want to get it the same way I did. You want it handed to you."

"You're wrong about that," Fine said. "We're willing to do whatever we gotta do."

"Except work for it," Gareth said. "I'm not trying to wind you up. I'm just making an observation. Why don't we get back to business for a minute? Let's settle the details and then we can party properly. Did you know I own a bar?"

Billy moved from under Gareth's arm and took Rick by the hand, drawing him a few feet away. "I hate listening to Gareth talk business," Billy said, as he leaned on one of the heavy wrought-iron tables.

Rick was very interested in Gareth's business, but he could see what was going down, and he'd find out all about it soon enough. His thoughts still swirled around the bombing and it was difficult to keep his mind on the here and now, to keep his emotions under control. He wanted to confront Hairy Carey, but knew that Gracie's advice was good. Though it chafed him, Rick knew he had to wait.

"That dork Fine thinks you're having it off with Gareth too," Billy baited Rick.

"So what?" Rick said.

"It doesn't bother you that that junior-league Al Capone thinks you're a sperm bank?"

"Why should it? He doesn't know me and it's not true."

Billy looked at Rick over the top of his sunglasses. "You're very centered," he said sarcastically. "Will you be my guru?"

"I'm still wondering," Rick changed the subject. "Why do you do this?"

"Gareth can give me what I need," Billy said.

"And what's that? Money? Drugs? Humiliation?"

"You think I'm ashamed of my role?"

"You're the one that mentioned sperm banks, so how could you not be? Take this little scenario for instance: Did Gareth ask you to be at the meeting, or did he bring these guys to the pool because you were here already?"

"What?"

"Don't pretend you don't know how you're being used. You're keeping those little maniacs distracted while Gareth does business with them."

"You're assuming they're gay."

"They're predators," Rick said flatly. "Any one of them would jump you in a second if they thought you were vulnerable. And

Gareth's giving them that impression in living color. The one with the rabid puppy-dog eyes was fantasizing about you out loud a few minutes ago."

"Then I guess I'm doing my job well," Billy said coolly.

Rick's gaze narrowed as he looked away from the young man. "You know, you walk and talk just like a hard-shelled whore, but every now and then, I see flashes of something else. Not right now, of course, but every now and then. So why doesn't it bother you to give yourself to someone like Carey?"

"I'd like to say it's because you don't know me and it's not true," Billy answered. "But I can't. I'm afraid I'm one of those people that make their bed but won't lie in it. I want to try to make a better bed. It really seems to upset the people around me."

"That makes two of us," Rick said unexpectedly. "I guess it would be hypocritical of me to look down on you."

"I wouldn't mind you looking down on me in the right circumstances," Billy said, tilting his face to a provocative angle.

"You can't help it, can you?" Rick finally smiled. "You have to seduce everyone."

"Look, stud," Billy said, straightening up as if for inspection. "This is what I've got to work with, okay? I wouldn't want my equipment to get rusty from lack of use."

"Ah, now I get it. Gareth is just practice for the big leagues."

Billy hid his smile by looking away from Rick and his glance fell by chance on Novacelli. Their eyes brushed for an immeasurably small fraction of time before Billy's gaze was veiled by his lashes, but

65

Novacelli stood stunned by Billy's smile, imagining that it was directed at him.

"Being with Gareth allows me to do what I want to do," Billy said.

"And what's that? Shopping? Hanging out with dangerous men? Getting smacked around?"

Billy's head came up sharply. Rick couldn't see the young man's eyes behind the dark sunglasses, but Billy's mouth was a grim line. Neither noticed Gareth arrive.

"Shite, Rick!" Gareth said. "What did you say to Billy? That's the look that says 'you aren't getting any tonight, Sunshine.' Sorry I missed it."

Rick glanced over at the group around the bar and changed the subject. "What the hell kind of name is Kookie Kutter Krew?"

Billy gave a short laugh. "Cookie is slang for a couple of things. I think it came from Pac-Man, but I don't really know. A cookie is a reward. It could be your paycheck, a bonus, sex, anything desirable, I guess."

Rick shook his head. "Do they realize that spelling it with a K makes it slang for crazy?"

Billy looked over at the Krew. "I have a feeling they do," he said. "Have you ever seen a bigger load of dags?"

"Be nice, Billy," Gareth said. "Daddy's doing business with these wannabes. In fact, it would be very nice of you to come and have a drink to celebrate our new partnership."

Billy pushed his sunglasses up on his head. "Partnership?"

Gareth shrugged. "You know how it is when you're wheeling and dealing, tiger kitten. Words get tossed around. Partnership can mean a lot of different things to different people. The point is, and you will appreciate this, the Krew are so enchanted with the idea of rubbing shoulders with real criminals that they've offered to sweeten the deal."

"You're kidding," Rick blurted out.

"It was their idea," Gareth said, barely suppressing his grin until he turned his back on the Krew. "I'm so lucky I ran into these...what did you call them, Billy?"

"Posers."

"Yes, that's it. I'm lucky I ran into these posers before someone else                                                                                     did."


"Yeah, just imagine how High-Tone would have handled this," Rick said.

Gareth's smile stayed on his lips, but his eyes lost their warmth. "What does that mean?"

"Gareth," Billy said. "I don't think Rick meant to criticize how you run things."

"Really? Because that's what it sounded like," Gareth said. "Why are you bringing up our former business partner, Rick?"

"Just making conversation," Rick said. "Didn't know the subject was off-limits."

"What were you going to say?" Gareth asked.

"High-Tone would never have met with these guys. He would have sent soldiers to kill them and take the drugs."

"I thought of that," Gareth said. "But I think they have more than they're telling us. Speaking of which…. Billy? Are you going to join us? And be friendly?"

Billy lifted his glass to his lips and drained the contents in several long swallows. Rattling the ice in the empty glass, he smiled at Gareth. "I seem to need a drink," Billy said. "You're coming too, Rick. You need a drink more than I do. Look at you. You look like you lost your best friend."

Rick glanced at the kid, but Billy had already put on his party face. The sparkling eyes and broad white smile would no doubt fool the Krew, but Rick saw how worn the mask was. Just under the layer of captivating glamour was weary resignation as deep as the Marianas Trench. Rick had seen it before. If Billy didn't leave this lifestyle soon, he'd end up at the bottom of the pool, or worse.

As Gareth and Billy charmed the Kutters, Rick found himself standing behind the bar next to Paul Macross. Levere, playing waiter, came over with a drink order. After listening to Levere's terse, unflattering assessment of their gangbanger wannabe guests, Rick asked where Geordie was.

"He's visiting some contacts in the city," Levere said. "Wonder how long Gareth expects us to act chummy with these arseholes?" Paul handed Levere a serving tray laden with bottles and ice-filled glasses. "Fuck!" Levere exclaimed as the tray started to tilt. Rick put out a hand and balanced it until Levere got hold of it again. "Thanks, mate," Levere said. "I'm not a bloody waiter."

"Then what are you doing carrying drinks?" Macross asked.

Levere cocked an eyebrow and then shoved the tray back to Paul. "Here you go, sport," he said. "You're better at this than me."

"No problem," Macross answered. "At least now the guests have some hope of drinking these instead of wearing them."

"Dickheads," Levere said darkly, eyeing their guests as Macross walked away.

"Do you know what game Gareth is playing with them?" Rick asked.

"Don't care," Levere said. "They might end up staying the night if they keep entertaining the boss. If they do, I'm definitely shagging that blond one. I've never fucked a boy named Flip before."

"I wish I had your ambition."

"I know you think I'm a Neanderthal, and maybe you're right, but I can tell when someone's taking the piss with me, and I don't much like it."

"Don't sell yourself short," Rick said. "You're a Cro-Magnon, at least."

Levere cracked a smile. "Good one," he said. "And look, I think the children are finally going home."

Rick glanced over as Gareth walked away with the Kutters, Macross and Epiphano trailing them like Dobermans. Billy came over and leaned on the bar. Picking up the vodka bottle, he splashed some in his glass. "Rick," he said. "Walk me to my room?"

Levere's look of surprise went unnoticed by the other two men.

"Sure," Rick said. "You ready now?"

Billy nodded. "I need a shower. Letting sweaty-handed half-grown trendoids paw at me has left me feeling…grungy is the word, I guess."

"I could help with that," Levere said.

"No, you couldn't," Billy answered. "Come on, Rick."

Rick stopped at the door of Billy's room and said good night. Billy gave Rick another of his complex looks and before Rick could react, the young man had swooped close and kissed him. After the shock wore off, Rick took Billy by the biceps and held him away.

"What the hell do you think you're doing?" Rick asked. "You want to get me fired? Or killed?"

Billy rolled his eyes. "I don't think Gareth cares anymore. If he did, he surely would have caught me by now. I've been prolifically unfaithful."

"Then how about asking me if I want to kiss you?"

"Touché," Billy said softly. "You stopped me cold with that one. All right then; I'll say good night. I just wanted to thank you for being there tonight."

"I wish I could say it was my pleasure."

"If I wasn't so drunk, I'd never tell you this, but for whatever reason you're here," Billy said even more softly. "I'm glad."

Rick stared at the closed door for a long moment before he went to the other wing of the big house and lay down on his bed. He had acted cool, and he thought Billy had bought his act, but Rick couldn't fool himself. Laying here in the darkness with only his thoughts for company, Rick's mind returned again and again to the moment when

Billy's mouth had touched his. He could still feel the warm silkiness and gentle pressure of those sweet lips before they seemed to meld with his. Of their own volition, Rick's fingers curled around his stiffening shaft, but he released it, turned onto his side, and punched his pillow into shape. He was not going to think about Billy anymore tonight. He was going to sleep.

"HEY, tiger kitten," Gareth said as he came into Billy's room. "We are going to be very…well, even richer than we are. Does that make you happy?"

Billy smiled back at Gareth. "It makes me want to spend money," he said. "That's close enough to happy."

"It makes me horny," Gareth said. "Strip and get on the bed."

"Please," Billy said sarcastically. "Stop all the mushy stuff. It's embarrassing, really."

Gareth rolled his head on his neck. "Are we feeling cheeky?" he asked.

"I don't like being spoken to as if I were one of your shaved apes," Billy said.

"Why not?" Gareth said, cracking his knuckles as he came across the room. "You're all on the same payroll, aren't you?"

"Would you mind terribly if we skipped this tonight?"

"Terribly," Gareth answered, excitement growing as he scented something new in Billy's usual line of rebuff. "But feel free to resist as much as you like."

A brief eternity later, Gareth rose, stretched, and left without a word to sleep in his own room. Glad to be rid of Gareth's weight, Billy lay still a while longer, staring without seeing at the intricately carved molding that bordered the ceiling. Eventually, the minor aches and bruises, legacy of Gareth's so-called lovemaking, drove the young man from the comfort of his bed to the comfort of his bathroom. He filled the mammoth tub with steaming hot water and gingerly lowered himself into the scented depths. Jamming a rolled-up towel behind his neck, he tipped his head back, closed his eyes, and commanded his muscles to relax. The hot water, the silence, and the smell of lavender in the bath oil wove a soothing spell of tranquility that lulled Billy into a drowsy state. Neither awake nor asleep, neither dreaming nor scheming, he hovered between the real and the intangible, between what was and what had been, drifting easily into a memory that was a fantasy.

The bathroom door opened and Billy smiled a welcome at the man who stood in the opening. His visitor's pale hair was a halo of thatched tufts, evidence of its recent and prolonged contact with a pillow. A wide-mouthed yawn froze in surprise, and the man began to retreat with an apology for intruding. Billy held out a hand in tacit invitation. After a brief hesitation, the blond-haired man closed the door behind him and came across the room, shedding his pajama bottoms on the way. Naked, except for his freckles and a few patches of golden hair, he knelt beside the tub and leaned over it. Eyes closed, Billy raised his face, eager for the kiss, and felt the brush of something like the silken petals of a poppy.

Hungry for more, Billy wrapped a hand around the back of the other man's neck and welded their mouths together. The taste and the sensual slide of tongues ignited a craving that would not be denied. Clutching at his visitor's shoulders, Billy pulled him into the tub slowly, for he was reluctant to allow their lips to part. With much sliding of wet skin against wet skin, Billy maneuvered himself atop the other man. Only then did he break the epic kiss in order to sample various other bits for the first time. Dizzy with the sheer audacity of it, Billy licked, sucked, and nibbled his way along the strong jawline prickly with stubble, down the column of the neck, stopping to pay special attention to the tender hollows of the collarbones, before traversing the flat plane of a pectoral to the pink peak of a sensitive nipple. Teasing the hard bud with teeth and tongue, Billy captured its twin between his thumb and forefinger, rolling it gently. The blond-haired man moaned his approval, lifting his pelvis to press against Billy's. Billy arched his back, bringing his hard cock solidly athwart the other man's. Leaning in, he brought their mouths together in a deep kiss as he pulsed his arousal against his partner's hard length. Thrusting with tongues and cocks, the two men rocked together to the sound of miniature waves lapping against the sides of the tub. Faster and harder, they bucked in tandem, aching dicks rubbing, sliding, and rolling with just enough tantalizing friction to drive them to greater efforts in pursuit of more. Billy wasn't even sure it was possible to get enough of this, but for this man he was more than willing to give it his best shot.

Hips pumping, asses rising and falling, squeaking against porcelain, breaching the steamy air and diving again into the blood-hot water, they rubbed against each other until they struck a spark of an all-consuming blaze. The point had passed when fondling was enough; they needed to be closer, now, if not sooner. Billy rose to his knees, straddling his partner's hips and took hold of the other man's cock. Bringing the taut head to his opening, he lowered himself onto the hard shaft, sinking slowly down until half the length was snugly ensconced. The blond-haired man groaned in bliss, meeting Billy's gaze with a look of grateful wonder. Taking hold of Billy's yearning arousal, his lips parted to speak words of love.

This was the point at which Billy always became aware of his self-delusion, that he was on his knees in the tub jerking off, but he held on to the fragments of the fantasy for as long as he could. Tonight he was able to preserve the mood until he reached climax. He supposed he should be thankful for even the smallest favors as he strove to imagine his dream lover moving inside him, filling him to a completeness he'd never known, prodding him toward paradise with each stroke. Billy sank to a crouch as his orgasm bloomed in his lower belly and a jet of cum bloomed in the bathwater, atomic clouds of joy, with such a short half-life. After he came, he always remembered that this could only ever be a fantasy. It could never happen in real life. He was doomed to a soul-deep longing that would never be requited. It was best that he concentrate on the present and keep in mind that tender feelings were a weakness that led inevitably to regret of the worst kind. He carried with him the knowledge that his tragedy was of his own making; he had chosen and now nothing could ever be put right again. It was futile, but that knowledge wouldn't stop him from playing the game out to the end. After all, what else did he have?

Getting to his feet, Billy opened the drain and stepped from the tub as the water infused with his seed went swirling away. He toweled off and wiped the fog from the mirror. Sternly, he told his reflection to deal with the here and now and stop dreaming. His doppelganger looked suitably resolved, but as he turned to go to bed, he knew in his heart that the next time his dream lover appeared, he'd welcome him in every way he knew how. Once a fool, always a fool was what they'd carve on his headstone. There was no doubt his control was slipping, and just when he could least afford it.

# ~ Chapter Seven ~

"HOW did you sleep?" Geordie asked when Rick showed up in the gym's shower room the next morning.

Rick shook his head. His sleep had been filled with dreams of Billy; dreams that left him with linen to launder when he woke.

"That good, eh?" Geordie chuckled. "I've got news that should perk you up. We're going out later to pick up a sample of the product."

"Finally, some action," Paul Macross said as he came out of the showers and grabbed a towel.

"You want action?" Geordie said, openly admiring Paul's sculpted physique. "I'll give you action, boyo."

Paul did an Elvis roll of his hips and continued toweling off. "You couldn't handle me," he said.

"Not this early," Geordie agreed. "I'll see you when I get back though."

"You're not taking me along?" Paul pouted. "Shit!"

"Somebody has to hold down the fort," Geordie said. "And you're appointed."

"What about Rick?"

"Rick's coming with me," Geordie said. "I want to watch him work."

"Where and when?" Rick asked.

"We'll meet these losers at their clubhouse at two," Geordie said. "Gareth's decided he doesn't want them coming back here. Something about their manners he didn't like."

"I'll be ready," Rick said. "I'm going for a swim. See you later."

Geordie nodded as though granting permission and Rick left. After a few laps in the pool, the undercover cop went into the cabana to shower off the chlorine and change. As he entered the cool, shadowy interior, small wet noises echoed off the tile.

"Is someone in here?" Rick called.

"Uh, yeah. Just…. Just give me a minute."

Rick recognized Billy's voice and imagined the young man on his knees avidly mouthing Levere's dick. "No problem," he said loudly. "Sorry to interrupt."

"You're not…interrupting anything," Billy said, the hitch in his voice more pronounced.

Rick quelled the erotic visions and walked through the changing area. Billy looked up at the sound of Rick's footsteps. The young man's cheeks were wet and more tears overflowed the big doe eyes. Picking up the towel from his lap, Billy dabbed at his face and Rick did his best to ignore the fact that the young man was stark naked. He failed miserably. Knowing it was a mistake, but unable to stop, Rick knelt on the tile and took the kid in his arms. Billy leaned into Rick's comforting warmth and it seemed such a natural thing for Rick to lower his face and kiss those offered lips. The petal softness parted for him, and his tongue accepted the tacit invitation. Billy moaned softly and the sound triggered a sympathetic vibration in Rick's crotch. His cock roused and quivered in anticipation of imitating his tongue. It had been a long dry spell for Rick, and the desirable body in his arms was willing and pliant. For a brief eternity, lust overcame reason and Rick did as his instincts demanded. Billy pressed as close as he could to Rick's solidness as the man plundered his mouth. Weaving his fingers into Rick's sandy hair, the young man squeezed the undercover cop's rising crotch with the other hand. When Rick broke the kiss, Billy whimpered.

"Please don't stop. I love the way you kiss me. Kiss me again."

Rick complied gladly. He loved kissing—couldn't get enough of it—but his few lovers hadn't shared his passion for foreplay. His ex-wife had adored his skill and patience, but he always felt like he was going through the motions with her. He should've known then what he was, but it had taken nearly half his life to get comfortable with what he wanted.

Slipping his fingers under the waistband of Rick's trunks, Billy found the hot suede of the other man's arousal. With the ease of long practice, Billy stroked the thick shaft quickly to full erection. Using the fluid that seeped from the tip as lubricant, Billy pumped rapidly. Rick groaned as Billy explored his mouth while fondling his aching cock. Sliding his hands down Billy's back, Rick kneaded the firm buttocks. Billy moaned as Rick's fingers crept into his cleft and teased his opening. Nudging gently at the small rosette, Rick tongue-fucked

Billy's mouth as his dick slid against Billy's palm. Easing a finger past the resilient muscle that guarded the tight passage, Rick probed until Billy made a small hungry noise against his lips. Diligently rubbing the springy bump in the front wall of Billy's sheathe, Rick provoked a series of muffled moans from Billy's lips. Billy wrapped his hand around Rick's arousal and his own, rubbing them together until he came with a strangled cry and a convulsive shudder. His fist tightened and he bit at the other man's lower lip as his climax unfurled. Rick's fingers sank into the tanned skin of Billy's ass, as he thrust into the kid's clenched fingers. Billy twisted his wrist at the top of his stroke, flicking his thumb over the seeping head of Rick's cock. Sensing imminent release, he sucked hard on the other man's tongue. Rick came so hard he was afraid he was going to black out. Swaying slightly, he put his palms on the floor, lowering Billy to his back on the tile. The young man closed his eyes and turned his face away, as Rick caught his breath.

"Holy…shit," Rick panted into Billy's ear. "I can't…believe…I…"

"Billy! Where the fuck are you, you gorgeous pain in the ass?" Gareth called out.

Rick froze for a moment while Billy scrambled out from under him. Wiping his fingers on the towel, the young man ran for the shower and turned it on. Rick gave the kid an apologetic look as Billy shooed him fiercely toward the back of the pool house.

"Is my tiger kitten all lathered up?"Gareth asked as he entered the locker room.

"I'm taking a shower; what do you think?" Billy said over the noise of the water.

"I'll be right in to wash your back," Gareth said.

Billy leaned against the tiled wall with his eyes closed remembering how it had felt to have Rick's arms around him. In another life, maybe he could have someone like Rick, but not in this one. In this life, he got Gareth Carey, who was about to fuck him with no lube but crème rinse, he was betting. And Billy would take it. Because to refuse would arouse the creep's suspicions and Gareth was paranoid enough as it was. Telling himself for the millionth time that it would be worth it in the end, Billy opened his eyes.

Gareth finished undressing and stroked his cock a few times. Gritting his teeth, Billy tensed as the other man stepped into the shower stall with him. It was a large area, but with Gareth standing behind him, Billy couldn't turn without brushing against him. However, if he didn't turn, his back would be to Gareth. *What difference does it really make,* Billy thought, as he lifted his face to the spray.

"Was there someone in here before I came in?"Gareth asked as his hands settled on Billy's shoulders.

"What do you mean?"

"You know, Billy," Gareth said, wrapping his fingers around the young man's slender neck, "answering a question with a question is a classic stall for time. Why would you need to think about it?"

"Because you're a sadistic paranoid freak?"

Gareth grabbed one of Billy's wrists and yanked it up between the young man's shoulder blades. Pushing Billy against the tile, Gareth pressed his erection to the firm buttocks.

"Nice and slippery," Gareth said, sliding his hard-on in the soapy groove.

"Are you trying to break my wrist?" Billy asked between clenched teeth.

"I think what I'm doing is technically called frottage," Gareth said. "But you're the expert on sex, baby-snakes. A fact I'm sure that Rodge appreciates."

"What's Roger Levere got to do with anything?"

"He's been wearing a peculiar smirk for the last week or so," Gareth said. "I finally identified it. It's the look that says I'm putting one over on the boss."

"And of course that means he's fucking me," Billy said.

Gareth eased the pressure on the young man's wrist. "If I thought he was shagging you, he'd be dead already," Gareth said. "I thought you knew the rules, but I guess I'll have to explain them again."

Billy sighed in relief as Gareth released his arm. It was still trapped between their bodies, but the excruciating pain was gone. He wasn't surprised when Gareth put an arm around his neck, but he didn't much like this position. It made him feel a bit too vulnerable, as if Gareth truly did have control of him.

Gareth put his free hand on the back of Billy's head and pressed his cheek to the cool ceramic. "Spread your legs," he said.

Billy widened his stance and braced himself as Gareth found his lower opening with an insistent finger. The young man couldn't hold in a whimper as he was roughly penetrated.

"Still bothers you, does it?" Gareth said. "You can't ever give it up easy, can you?"

"It hurts," Billy said succinctly.

"Oh, do pardon me," Gareth said, pushing his finger a little deeper.

"At least spit on it, you bastard," Billy said.

Gareth found the young man's prostate and circled it, pressing lightly. "You never cum when we're fucking," he said. "So I'm going to make sure you do this time."

"Stop it," Billy said, as the first flutters of arousal tightened his groin.

"That sounded like an order," Gareth said, tightening his arm around Billy's throat.

"You are such an arsehole," Billy wheezed.

"Tell me something I don't know," Gareth said, sliding his hard flesh up and down Billy's thigh, as he fingered him. "You brought this on yourself, my red angel. I know a cock-hungry, cum-drunk slut like yourself is bound to stray, but you need to learn that you cannot use my soldiers as your private stud farm. I can't have them forming attachments. Understand?"

Billy sucked in a deep breath as the pressure on his windpipe eased. "I understand that you're an insecure, thick-skulled bully," he gasped.

"And you are one sexy bitch," Gareth growled, massaging Billy's prostate with two fingers.

"Stop it!" Billy said. "I don't want you to do that."

Gareth's ears pricked up and his cock jerked at the new note in his favorite toy's voice. Unable to wait any longer, Gareth withdrew his fingers and positioned his arousal at Billy's entrance. At an agonizingly slow pace, he pushed into the contracting passage. "I want to teach you a lesson," Gareth said, "but I don't want to take you to the emergency room, so you be sure and let me know if you feel anything tear."

Billy didn't answer; he was busy absorbing the pain of the penetration. Millimeter by millimeter the thick rod of flesh forced its way into him. Not until Gareth's balls were snugly against Billy's ass did forward motion stop. "You're mine," Gareth said in Billy's ear. "I might wink at small indiscretions, but if you step over the line again, you'll need a lot more than stitches to put you right."

Billy groaned as the big cock began backing out. A shiver of sheer erotic pleasure ran down Gareth's spine at the sound of misery. Bending over the young man's back, Gareth wrapped his arms around Billy and thrust powerfully. With his arms trapped at his sides, Billy strove to maintain control as Gareth pounded into him. Abruptly, it became too much and he began to struggle. Delighted, Gareth tightened his grip and pushed deeper.

"Stop it!" Billy cried, his voice echoing off the tile. "Get off me, Gareth!"

"Fuck! I'm going to explode," Gareth panted in the other man's ear. "Don't stop."

Billy thrashed in the big man's hold, throwing himself around to no avail. His flailing excited Gareth to a nearly unbearable degree, and the gangster gleefully reinserted his cock each time he was unseated.

As he felt his climax build to the point of no return, Gareth pressed Billy flat against the wall and sheathed his aching rod. Billy trembled with rage and pain as Gareth rolled his hips, shifting his cock minutely in the clenching passage. Desperately, the young man bore down on the shaft that impaled him, seeking to end Gareth's lesson quickly.

"Bloody hell, that feels incredible," Gareth groaned. Grasping Billy's slim hips with bruising force, Gareth dug his fingers into the soft flesh and thrust in short, sharp jabs. Billy began to whimper as the cruel hands moved to his ass and Gareth's thumbs sank into him along with Gareth's cock.

"I'll kill you for this someday," Billy told the man that abused him, horrified by the whining sound of his voice.

"I know you will, pet," Gareth said. "If I don't kill you first."

Billy closed his eyes as Gareth came with a rumbling groan of fulfillment. As his climax washed through him, Gareth ran his hands over Billy's chest and crotch, rubbing his coarse beard against the young man's nape. Willing it to be over, Billy remained still as the other man pawed at him in post-orgasmic bliss. When Gareth grasped at Billy's limp cock, Billy pushed him off with a convulsive shudder. Gareth landed on the tiled bench behind him and grinned up at his furious paramour. "You feel that?" Gareth's laugh bubbled out of his mouth. "That's a little bit of me way up inside you, marking you as mine. That really fucks with you, doesn't it, kitten?"

"You're a dead man," Billy said.

"We're all walking dead men," Gareth said. "Now keep your hands off the hired help. Especially the new guy."

Billy picked up the liquid soap and turned the hot water up. Having delivered his threat once again, he had nothing else to say to Gareth. Seeing that he'd get no further reaction from Billy, Gareth dressed and left.

RICK came from around the back of the pool house and entered the mansion through one of the French doors off the terrace. He had a bad moment when he saw Geordie standing there as though waiting for him. Rick couldn't be sure, but he figured Geordie had seen him walk up from the pool house, and Geordie almost certainly knew Gareth was there with Billy now.

"Come on," Geordie said impatiently. "Did you forget we have an appointment at two?"

Rick's heart rate went down as he realized Geordie wasn't being confrontational. "Hang on; I'll get my piece," he said.

Geordie nodded. "Go," he said. "But from now on, you stay packed, understand?"

"You got it, boss," Rick said as he walked away.

Rick wondered what was going through Geordie's head, but pushed it to the back of his mind. He needed to be sharp for this job, and he needed to talk to someone whose motivations he was sure of. As soon as he was out of the Brit's sight, Rick went out to the driveway and took out his phone. Quickly, he let Graciela know what was going down. She wished him luck and signed off with her usual warning to watch his ass.

Graciela put the phone down and looked at the men looming over her. "Everything's fine," she said. "You boys would be smart to just leave Rick where he is."

"Damn it, Gracie!" Captain Walter Little said. "I can't let Rick get away with this cowboy shit, and you want me to reward him."

"I fail to see how leaving him in a dangerous, potentially fatal situation qualifies as a reward, captain," said Chief Inspector Frehley.

"You don't know Rick, Inspector Frehley," Little sighed.

"I think you might call me Campbell since it seems we'll be working together for a time," the tall man said.

"In that case, I'm Walter and this lovely but misguided lady is Detective Graciela Cruz."

"Gracie," she said, giving the spit-polished Brit a megawatt smile and offering her hand. "I look forward to working with you, sir."

"Who says you aren't suspended?" Little asked.

"Now boss," Graciela said, "you know Rick won't work with anyone but me."

"True," Walter said, "but disciplinary action is only postponed. You and Rick are going to have to be reprimanded at the least."

Frehley made a sound suspiciously like a snort and both American cops turned to look at him. "Sorry; it's just that if one of my officers had taken this upon himself, he would no longer have a badge."

"Welcome to America," Graciela said. "Things are a little different here. We even have girl cops. Hope it doesn't wilt your stiff upper lip too much."

"I shall endeavor to cope," Campbell said solemnly, closing the door to the captain's office. "Now...shall we get down to brass tacks?"

"By all means," Graciela said. "I like a man that lays it out on the table."

"Gracie," Walter said. "Do I have to get the muzzle?"

"Sorry, sir," she said. "I'll be quiet while the men talk."

Campbell's wide mouth curved in a near-smile. "I like your spirit, young woman. Feel free to join the discussion...if you've anything to add."

Graciela nodded and squelched her next comment, which would've been a sarcastic offer to fetch coffee for them. Frehley probably drank tea anyway.

"As I earlier informed the captain," Campbell said, "I've lost touch with one of my men. This is of interest to you because the agent is working undercover to arrest Gareth Carey. You'll forgive me if I don't reveal his name, but the temptation to tell your partner would be too great, I'm afraid."

"Oops," Graciela said. "I told Rick this was a stupid thing to do, but I didn't know we'd be interfering with another investigation. You have my sincere apology for poaching."

"Accepted," Frehley said. "Now let us see what we may do to salvage the situation."

"Seems to me that if you told Rick who your man was, he could pass messages to him," Graciela said.

"So it would seem," Campbell agreed. "However, I think the risk of discovery would go up exponentially if the two men were aware of one another's identities."

Graciela frowned. "Really?"

"I'll make you the loan of a book that details the danger of accumulative activity and describes unconscious recognition signals, among other subjects."

"Sounds like psychology. Was it written by some shrink that never came near an undercover operation?"

"Actually, I wrote it," Frehley said. "From information gathered in years of field service. And for the record, I do have a degree in criminal psychology."

"Oops, again," Graciela said.

"You walked into that one, Gracie," her captain told her. "What can we do to help, Campbell?"

"We can use Detective Miles to keep track of my officer without either being aware of it as long as Detective Cruz consents to relay his conversations and ask him key questions."

"Of course," Graciela said. "I'm just wondering about one thing."

Both men looked at her inquiringly.

"Do we still get the collar?"

# ~ Chapter Eight ~

RICK pulled the glossy black SUV to the curb and cut the engine. Dubiously, he looked down the block at the hangar-sized building. It was near the docks but not close enough that there was much foot traffic. The undercover cop did his best to scour his mind of all thoughts of Billy. He couldn't afford the distraction. However, the young man's scent seemed ingrained in the whorls of Rick's fingertips. *I should never have let things go that far,* he thought. *I must be insane. The kid is pure nitroglycerin. Shake him too hard and he'll explode, raining flaming debris on everyone.*

Still, Rick couldn't banish Billy entirely. How could he dismiss something that felt so right on an almost molecular level? When he remembered how they had meshed, flesh and spirit, he knew he'd had a preview of what the poets wrote about: a passion so all-consuming that it could not be denied or withstood. Which was just about the last thing Rick needed right now, though he yearned for it with all his heart.

*Get the kid out of your head,* Rick's interior voice ordered ruthlessly, *before you do something stupid.* "You sure this is the address?" Rick asked the man next to him.

Geordie checked the slip of paper in his hand. "Yeah. Figures they'd have their headquarters in some piece of shit warehouse. They probably think the waterfront address makes them look like bad-asses."

"Maybe it's their Bat Cave," Rick said, playing into Geordie's conversational gambit. Talking was good. It calmed the nerves and Rick didn't want a bunch of nervous gun-toting hoods standing close to him.

"Assholes," Epiphano muttered his opinion of the junior gangsters as he shoved his Glock into the back of his jeans.

Levere laughed. "Fucking assholes," he improved on Epiphano's observation.

Rick shoved another extra magazine into his pocket. The Kutters were not at all concerned about the law and they were still young enough to feel immortal, a deadly combination. "So now that we've all decided we don't like them, I guess we won't be asking for any autographs. What do you say we get in there and get this over with?"

Geordie turned around to look at Levere and Epiphano in the backseat. "No shooting unless it's necessary," he said. "Understand?"

Levere and Epiphano looked at each other and smirked.

"Sure thing, boss," Epiphano said.

"No worries," Levere seconded his partner.

Geordie checked his ammo and shoved his Sig Sauer back into his shoulder holster before he pushed his door open. Rick joined him and the two of them started up the concrete walk side by side, with Levere and Epiphano behind them.

"I have the uncanny notion that shooting will become necessary," Levere whispered.

"Damn straight," Epiphano replied, butting his fist against Levere's.

"So how do you think this is going to go?" Geordie looked over at Rick.

"Badly," the undercover cop sighed.

"Yeah. Me too," Geordie said. "These Kutters just plain piss me off."

They came around the corner to a roll-up door guarded by a young man in a bomber jacket. Aware that Geordie was grading his performance, Rick spoke first.

"We're here to see Fine," Rick said.

The man-child looked them up and down with deliberate disdain. "You from Hairy Carey's gang?"

"No, you snot-nosed little ratbag. We're with Amway. Do you think anyone inside would like to see a demonstration of cleaning products?" Levere snarled.

"You wanna get me lathered up, pervert?" the kid sneered.

Rick held Levere back with an arm across the Aussie's barrel chest. "Gareth Carey sent us," he said. "And if I were you I'd forget about that colorful nickname. Now, is your boss here?"

"Aren't you supposed to have a case full of money for him?"

Rick shook his head at this impudence. "What's your name?"

"Ask your mama," the teenager sneered.

Rick grabbed a handful of jacket and pinned the punk against the door. "Listen up, asswipe. We don't have any money with us because we're not buying until we're sure of the quantity of the product. Now stop playing the negotiator and take us inside, or I'll let my excitable friend here have a go at convincing you. I promise you that you don't want that. He's not nearly as civilized as I am."

The kid's eyes darted to Levere. The burly Australian looked as though taking a piece out of some punk's ass was all he wanted for Christmas. "I'm Cody," the sentry said. "Follow me, and I'll take you to Nate."

Rick walked into the warehouse behind the kid, wondering again if the case was worth what he'd lost thus far in pursuing it. He was beginning to feel like a short fuse on a hinky stick of TNT. Flexing his hands, he tried to center himself as Cody stopped at the door leading into a complex of offices.

"In there," the lookout said sullenly, pointing to an interior door. Through the opening, they could see Nathan Fine sitting at a battered desk.

"No, you need to come back now," the Kutters' leader barked into his phone.

Cody knocked on the doorframe. "Carey's men are here," he said as though announcing the arrival of IRS agents.

Geordie and Rick didn't wait to be asked, muscling past the kid into the room. "I know you wouldn't want to keep us waiting," Geordie said.

Fine closed his cell phone and looked up from behind a desk cluttered with X-rated comic books, overflowing ashtrays, and convenience store coffee cups. Through the large plate-glass window behind Fine, Rick could see Flip Hudson in some sort of break room playing cards with three other young men. Rick looked for the creep, but Rafe Novacelli wasn't there. The little tweaker's absence struck Rick as fundamentally wrong; Rafe was Nate Fine's dog and should be at his master's side.

"Greetings, gentlemen. Please take a seat," Fine said grandly as Epiphano and Levere filled the doorway behind Cody. "Is there anything my man can get for you? A drink? A smoke? A woman? No problem."

Fine's exaggerated congeniality rang alarm bells with Rick. There was definitely something wrong with this picture, but he couldn't see it yet. "This isn't a social call, Fine," he took the initiative. "Mr. Carey may be entertained by your bullshit, but not me. Who was that on the phone?"

"That was Rafe, if it's any of your business. Are you sure you wouldn't like a little something while we wait?"

"You heard Rick; let's get this over with," Geordie joined the conversation.

Rick glanced significantly at Epiphano and Levere. Epiphano slid back into the hallway and away from the door, as Levere trained his eyes on the card players. Neither Cody nor Fine reacted to the ramped-up level of alertness; people were always nervous around large piles of cash, or narcotics. The punks' failure to respond spoke of supreme confidence or an overwhelming naiveté. Neither option made Rick feel any better.

"Understood," Fine replied, pushing his chair back as he stood up. "If you gentlemen will just follow me?" Nathan came around the desk and Geordie allowed the kid to precede them out of the room. Rick and Geordie exchanged a look that confirmed that neither felt comfortable with Fine's insouciant master of ceremonies demeanor. The atmosphere in the Kutters' clubhouse was a little too laid back to be genuine.

"Be ready," Rick whispered to Geordie. "I'm getting the distinct feeling that we're not far from a world of shit."

"I feel it too," Geordie muttered. "Weird tension."

As they filed into the room where the card game was going on, Hudson looked up and placed his cards face down on the table. The other players reminded Rick of a pack of strays just waiting for the alpha dog to slip up so they could tear him apart. Not the sorts that were long on loyalty, these guys were obviously in it for the money. Rick figured the odds at about fifty-fifty that these hired guns would fire or put down their weapons if the situation devolved into gunplay.

Fine unlocked the door behind Flip and Geordie followed him inside. "Nice," Rick heard Geordie say, "but where's the rest?"

"I ain't that clueless," Fine answered. "If I tell you that, what would you need me for?"

93

"Gareth sent us here to confirm the quantity. He's going to be very disappointed."

"Tell him we've got all he can handle; he has my word on it."

Geordie laughed. "Your word? Aren't you the same bloke that told us the shit was here?"

Rick looked through the doorway. "Give us a break, Fine. We can't go back and tell Gareth that he has your word. Why don't you just show us a brick or two and we'll be on our way?"

"That just isn't possible right now," Fine admitted reluctantly.

Rick saw something in Geordie's eyes shift and the hair on the back of his neck stood up. Edging carefully aside as Fine and Geordie walked out past him, Rick realized that the card game had ended. Epiphano was still in the hallway and Levere stood next to Cody, who had his hands in his jacket pockets. Fine stopped at Hudson's shoulder, and gave the visitors the bottom line.

"You've got my word," he said. "You can leave with that, or you can just leave."

"Fine," Rick said. "The deal is off. We're out of here."

"The fuck it is," Cody said, pulling a nine-millimeter. "You assholes aren't going anywhere."

# ~ Chapter Nine ~

IN his peripheral vision, Rick could see Epiphano easing forward and shook his head, warning him off. If shooting could still be avoided, he would do his best to prevent it.

"Look, kid," Rick said. "We're leaving here. The rest is between your boss and mine."

"I'm the only one holding a gun," Cody said. "I'll give the orders."

"You forgot to say nobody moves and nobody gets hurt," Rick said. "If you're going to talk in clichés, you might as well use them all."

"You dissin' me, Dad?" Cody asked.

"Duh," Levere said. "You shit-for-brains pillow-biter."

Cody turned his gun on Levere. "What the hell does that mean?"

"You'd be a lot happier riding my pole, peg boy."

"Fuck you, shithead!" Cody shouted.

Hudson shoved his chair back, and the others at the table stood up. Cody was no longer the only one with a gun in his hand.

"Don't make this happen, Cody," Rick said and the kid's gun swung back to him.

Geordie pointed his Sig at Cody. "Let it go," he told the Kutters. "You pups are courting a variety of trouble way beyond your reckoning."

Cody hesitated, glancing aside at Levere, as the potential for violence balanced on a scalpel's edge. Levere winked and blew Cody a kiss. The kid's finger tightened reflexively on the trigger and the sleek automatic began to spit bullets. Hudson shoved the unarmed Fine out of his line of fire as Levere and Epiphano drew and fired as one. Rick and Geordie rolled to the left as the shots rang out. Cody, still spraying lead, was rounding on Levere and Epiphano as they separated and flanked him.

"Cease firing!" Rick yelled at the room at large.

Cody's head whipped around along with the nine mil. Rick fired and a bullet meant to disarm hit nearly dead center in the kid's chest. The young man hit the floor, his gun falling from his limp fingers, as Rick and Geordie crawled across the floor using the scattered chairs and boxes as cover. Two of the four poker players were down and showing no signs of life; only Flip Hudson was still exchanging fire with Levere and Epiphano. Geordie pulled on Rick's arm, pointing toward the hallway.

"I can't see Fine," Rick said.

"Forget him. You head toward the door; I'll cover you," Geordie replied.

"What about you?" Rick asked.

"I'm going after Fine."

"You just said to forget him. Come on. We can both make it to the door."

"This is personal," Cook said, as he reloaded. "I owe Fine and I intend to pay up."

"You're crazy," the undercover cop said.

"No one's perfect. Now get the hell out of here. I'll meet you by the car."

Rick stared at Geordie until the man began laying down covering fire. Crouching low, Rick snapped off a couple of shots as he broke from hiding. Levere and Epiphano added their support as Rick dove toward the hall. Epiphano reached around the doorframe and yanked the running man to safety. A red handprint stained Rick's sleeve where Epiphano had grabbed him.

"Are you hit, or is that someone else's blood?" Rick asked.

Epiphano stepped back, ignoring the question, giving Rick his spot at the door as he pulled a clip from his pocket. "This is it," Epiphano said. "I'm empty after this."

"We got everyone except Hudson," Levere yelled over the racket.

Geordie slung a folding chair toward the table Hudson crouched behind, knocking it over. Levere and Rick fired in tandem, hitting

Hudson several times. The baby-faced thug went down, but not before emptying his weapon. Levere was hit in the throat and fell back, choking on his own blood. Epiphano slid to the floor and tried to pull Levere into the hallway. A round ricocheted off the far wall and hit him in the temple. Epiphano slumped over Levere's body and didn't move again.

Rick looked down at the dead men and held on to his detachment. The hollow clank of his empty clip hitting the concrete floor sounded as an anvil dropped from a third story window as he peered around the doorframe. Slamming a fresh load into the butt of the gun, he eased out into the room. Hudson raised himself up on his elbow and pointed his weapon at Rick. As a bullet whined past his ear, Rick put a round into Hudson's forehead, knocking him backward.

"Nice shot."

Rick swung to meet the threat, relaxing when he recognized Geordie's voice.

"Fine?" Rick asked tersely as Geordie trotted over to him.

"Not so fine," Cook said. "He won't be any more bother to us. Let's get out of here."

Rick hurried after Geordie, but slowed as he reached Cody's body. Though Rick had accepted the risks that came with undercover work, it hadn't occurred to him that he might be called upon to shoot children. He told himself that any one of these boys would have killed him with blinking, but somehow it didn't help. Kneeling, he closed the kid's eyes and jumped when they sprang open again.

"Asssss…hole," Cody exhaled wetly.

"What?"

Cody bared bloody teeth in a mocking red smile. "We could've," he coughed. "Could've owned this town with those Mexicans outta the way."

"Are you talking about Marcial?" Rick demanded, grabbing Cody by the jacket.

"Smoked 'em good. Rafe's the bomb."

Racking coughs shook Cody's body as he spewed blood, and Rick realized the dying punk was laughing. "What the fuck are you saying?" the undercover cop shouted. "Did Novacelli have something to do with Marcial's death?"

"Blew 'em up real good," Cody coughed again, disgorging another torrent of blood.

The kid's head drooped and his gaze grew fixed. Rick lowered the lifeless body to the floor as he absorbed the fact that the Kutters had taken out Antonio Marcial.

"What are you doing?" Geordie turned, grabbing Rick's arm and pushing Cody's body away. "Let's get the fuck out of here before the cops show up."

The two men ran from the warehouse to their waiting vehicle. Geordie stuck out his hand and Rick tossed him the keys, hanging on tight as Cook spun a smoking three-sixty and gunned the engine.

"Too bad about Levere and Epiphano," Geordie said tersely. "They were solid blokes."

The irony of the comment would have had Rick laughing if the situation weren't so fucked up. Levere and Epiphano were dead; they'd just blown away a gang barely old enough to shave, and once

Gareth heard their news, the bloodbath was sure to continue. Add to those facts a missing member of the Kutter gang who reputedly liked to play with explosives and the future had a distinctly dark tint.

"Slow down," Rick said abruptly.

"What?" Geordie asked.

Rick turned and looked pointedly at Geordie. "Slow down; we're going too fast and attracting attention that we don't need."

Geordie eased up on the pedal, looking from side to side as though he expected a police cruiser to materialize out of thin air. As they took the ramp onto the freeway, he pulled out his cell phone. "Gareth? Yeah, it's me. We're coming in two light and the package wasn't at the post office." The phone snapped shut and Geordie got into the right lane to take the exit that would lead them away from the industrial district.

"I assume he's less than happy," Rick commented.

Geordie barked out a laugh at Rick's words. "Mate, that's an understatement of epic proportion."

Rick couldn't help thinking about Billy right then. Gareth was royally pissed and it was almost impossible not to imagine him taking out his frustration on the kid. As was becoming his habit of late, Rick resolutely pushed the image from his mind. Things were going to happen fast from here on out and he needed time to think about his next move. How could he explain to his partner about being involved in something resembling the gunfight at the OK Corral?

"Relax," Geordie said as he pulled into the drive. "Gareth will know you held up your end."

"Thanks," Rick replied, as the aftereffects of the adrenaline rush hit him like a runaway cement mixer. His legs felt like jelly; he was sweating profusely, and his stomach was churning like pea soup on the boil. No wonder the other man was moved to offer him some reassurance. As Geordie shut his door, Rick took a deep breath and got out of the SUV. The first order of business was reporting to Gareth. If he survived that, then he'd think about throwing up.

# ~ Chapter Ten ~

"WHAT the fuck?" Gareth screamed as he lashed out viciously, backhanding Geordie across the jaw. Cook's head rocked on his neck, but he stood his ground. Gareth drew back his hand again, but let it fall to his side without striking another blow. "No fucking point in smacking you," he said furiously. "You hardly notice it."

Rick stiffened involuntarily, prepared to fight, as Gareth turned on him.

"Shit!" the crime boss shouted at the ceiling. "I am standing knee-deep in it and it's rising!"

"Then let's pick up some shovels," Rick said.

Gareth's incendiary gaze fastened on Rick's guileless blue eyes. Rick stared back with a calm he didn't feel. The undercover cop counted ten heartbeats before Gareth's contorted features relaxed into a neutral expression.

"You're right," Gareth said coolly. "We need to start shoveling. Before I became the successful man you see before you, I did my own dirty work. I fancy I haven't lost my touch just yet, and I think that this pile of shit needs my personal attention."

"Steady on," Geordie said. "No need for that. Rick and I put paid to those infant hooligans. They're grease spots on their own clubhouse floor."

Gareth swung his attention to his lieutenant. "That's very nice, Geordie," he said, his voice gaining volume with each word. "But where are my fucking drugs?"

Gareth hadn't mentioned the loss of Epiphano and Levere since Geordie had first informed him of their deaths, but Rick wasn't surprised. The missing narcotics were priority one. Gareth could always hire more meat; quality chemicals were a bit harder to come by. The boss's mood was swinging back to rage again, and Rick did his best to divert it.

"We'll find the product," he said. "One of the Kutters was conspicuous by his absence. I think those punks were a little smarter than they looked and took out some insurance."

Gareth's eyes narrowed in thought as he stared unseeing into the middle distance. Geordie caught Rick's gaze just as his pager vibrated against his thigh. Taking the small device from his pocket, Geordie looked at the number on the tiny screen. Instantly, the big man reached for his cell phone.

"What?" Gareth asked sharply.

Geordie spoke as he punched a number in speed dial. "It's Paul," he said.

The phone only rang once before Paul Macross answered, but the room grew extraordinarily still in that time. Rick could feel the atoms of air pressing against his skin as the tension drew tighter with each passing second.

"Paul, what the fuck?" Geordie shouted. "Bloody fucking hell! You better be taking the piss! What? Fuck me! Tell me how…"

Gareth snatched the phone from Geordie's hand and brought it to his ear. "Paul. It's Gareth. Slowly and carefully, tell me what the fuck is going on."

Several long moments later, Gareth spoke. "I see," he said with eerie calmness. "And I understand why you couldn't call earlier. Check yourself out as soon as you feel able and come straight home."

Gareth flipped the phone closed and tossed it at Geordie. Neither Geordie nor Rick spoke until Gareth did. The man's serenity was even more bizarre in light of what he told them.

"Paul's been shot and Billy's been abducted," Gareth said. "Taken right off the street by your missing Kutter, Rick, as it happens. Funny, but one doesn't expect this sort of thing in real life. In cliché action films perhaps, but not in real life."

"That little psycho Novacelli was drooling over Billy the night the Kutters were here," Rick said. "But since that's what you wanted, I didn't mention it."

"So I've bitten myself in the arse? Is that your point?" Gareth asked.

"Whoa, boss," Rick said. "I just wish I'd been sharper. We don't need to be arguing about it now, anyway. Let's go get Billy back."

"You have some idea how we can find him?" Geordie spoke up. "Because I sure as hell don't."

Rafael Novacelli dropped his phone into one of the many zippered pockets on his baggy jacket. "Nobody's answering me," he said despondently, but a glance at his passenger restored Novacelli's elation. The young man handcuffed to the door of the old Lincoln recoiled when the drug dealer reached toward him. "Aw, don't be like that," Novacelli said. "I'm a nice guy. I won't hurt you. That dude you were with would hurt you plenty though. He's got cold eyes. My dad had eyes like that and he was a hateful bastard."

Billy stared at the lunatic that had dragged him into a car on a city street in broad daylight after gunning down his bodyguard. His brain wanted him to look out the window and take note of their route, but his survival instinct kept his eyes on the driver.

"Hey, you can call me Rafe, if you want," Novacelli said with a shy smile. "That's what my buds call me."

"Rafe," Billy said carefully, "where are we going?"

"Well, I can't get Nate or Flip on the phone, which probably means something bad happened when your guys stopped by," Novacelli said glumly. "I should find out."

Billy shivered as the driver turned and a moist gaze crawled over him again. "Why don't you drop me off somewhere and go check on your friends?" he suggested. "I don't mind waiting until you get back."

"I can't let you go," Novacelli said reasonably. "You'd just go back to that mean dude. I can't let that happen."

"Rafe, think about this," Billy said softly. "You shot a man on the street in front of several witnesses. This car is hardly inconspicuous. You're going to get caught if you keep driving, and if I'm still with you, you'll go away for kidnapping. That carries the same sentence as murder, you know."

"Oh no," Novacelli said, smiling at Billy. "Don't you worry about that. The cops'll never get us."

"You sound awfully sure," Billy said.

Novacelli's smile became a sheepish grin. "I forgot; you don't know anything about me yet. I'm real good at making things. There's something I made in the backseat, if you want to look at it."

Billy had the sinking feeling that he would find nothing good when he looked over his shoulder. "Bloody hell," the young man muttered. "Why am I always right about the wrong thing?"

The device was immediately recognizable from its many appearances in popular cinema. Billy's gaze traveled over the disparate components—the timer, detonator, and explosive material connected by wires—and immediately identified the arrangement of hardware as a bomb. To his great relief, the numbers on the digital counter were static.

"You'd blow yourself up to avoid capture?" Billy asked numbly.

Novacelli reached into the small pocket inside his bomber jacket. With a proud smile, he displayed an oblong object made of black plastic about twice the size of a disposable lighter. Two tiny buttons and an ultra-slim antenna were the only significant features of the device. Billy recognized it instantly as a wireless transmitter. The lack of a red light on the end told him it wasn't infrared and didn't require line of sight to trigger the detonator. He wondered just what sort of range the remote had and it occurred to him that there was no harm in asking, given his current situation.

"What kind of range does that thing have?"

Novacelli beamed, beside himself with delight. His angel not only knew what he was holding; the desirable one was interested. This was a first in Novacelli's experience where the norm ran from yawning disinterest to violent rejection of his overtures. "I got this off the Internet," he said eagerly. "It's made from components for remote-controlled model airplanes. The range is awesome. You could be on the other side of a football field and still make contact. Farther probably."

"That is awesome," Billy said, glancing nervously into the backseat as they hit a bump. "How much explosive is that bad boy packing?"

"Don't worry," Novacelli said evasively. "I won't let us be taken alive."

"THAT'S plain daft," Geordie objected to Rick's theory.

"Sure is," Rick agreed without rancor. "But so is Novacelli."

"It really doesn't make sense," Gareth said. "Why would this arsehole take Billy back to the warehouse?"

"Because he doesn't know what happened yet," Rick said reasonably.

"But when he sees the mess we left, he'll scarper pretty damn quick," Geordie said. "Likely all we'll find is Billy's beautiful corpse. Sorry, Gareth."

"No harm, mate," Gareth said. "I'm not yet convinced that my tiger kitten isn't somehow in on this. He hooked me up with these punks. Maybe he set all this up to fuck with me for…" Gareth paused. "So tell us, Rick, why would Novacelli stay at the warehouse?"

"Because he's crazy," Rick said, "but he's not completely stupid. He'll figure the warehouse is the last place we'll look for him."


BILLY looked around in dismay at the crumpled bodies lying in large puddles of blood on the warehouse floor. "We can't stay here," he blurted out.

"Sure we can," Novacelli said. "This is the last place anyone will look for us now."

"Can we at least go to another room or something?"

Novacelli looked at Billy blankly for a long moment before comprehension sparked in his damp eyes. "Sure," he said. "This is kinda gross, huh?"

"Yeah… Gross," Billy echoed. It wasn't that he was the squeamish type; the copious gore, the flesh mutilated by high-speed projectiles didn't make him flinch. It was the wide-open eyes staring sightlessly into oblivion that made him uneasy. The light had gone out of their gazes, and once snuffed, it could not be rekindled. The thought put far too much perspective on his chosen lifestyle.

Novacelli took one of Billy's handcuffed wrists and tugged gently. "Come on," he said. "I'll show you my room." He took his captive up a short flight of stairs to what had once been an office above a row of lockable storage sheds inside the warehouse. It had a workbench along two walls overflowing with electronics in various stages of assembly. In one corner, makeshift shelves behind a stained mattress held a vast collection of triple X-rated paperbacks and glossy magazines. Aside from some large tool cabinets on wheels, the rest of the big space was virtually empty. "Do you like it?" Novacelli asked as he attached a chain to Billy's cuffs.

"It's…interesting," Billy said.

Novacelli clipped the leash to a heavy-duty clamp that secured the exposed ductwork in the ceiling. He then released one of Billy's hands from the cuffs. The chain was long enough to allow Billy to sit, or even lie down, without straining his arm, and he immediately did so. The drug dealer's mouth watered when his obsession sank down onto the mattress. This was going so well, he could hardly believe it. The bullet-riddled bodies of his friends might as well not have existed for all the thought he gave them. There was only one thing on his mind. "So…. You remember what you said to me at the party?" Novacelli asked.

Billy looked up in surprise. He couldn't remember what he'd said to any of the Kutters when they'd visited Gareth.

"At the party," Novacelli continued. "You asked me to…you know."

"I'm sorry," Billy said cautiously. "But I've forgotten what we talked about."

"That's impossible." A whiny note entered the other young man's voice. "You gotta remember!"

Billy swallowed hard and chose his words with care, aware that it would only take a single wrong one to set Novacelli off. "I told you I wanted to be with you," he guessed.

"Yesss!" Novacelli exulted. "I knew you didn't forget. You were just teasing me. Since you don't know me yet, you don't know that I don't like being teased."

"I promise I won't tease you again," Billy said with patent sincerity.

"Okay. So do you want to do that thing you said you wanted to do to me?"

"You know I do, Rafe," Billy said, hoping whatever this lunatic fantasized about wasn't too repellent. Billy had handled men that ran vast crime empires and ordered executions without blinking. Surely, he could placate this adolescent thug.

"You're so perfect," Novacelli said, gesturing to the manacles. "Sorry about those."

Billy looked at the chain that tethered him to the wall. "Don't worry about it," he said. "I like handcuffs."

Novacelli's eyes glowed like those of a Pekingese humping a favorite cushion. "I love you," he said diffidently.

"Of course you do," Billy said. "It's fate, isn't it? Higher forces and all that?"

"Yeah, that's right. We're destined to be together. It's so cool that you get it."

"Of course I do," Billy said wearily. "After all, I'm your soul mate, aren't I?"

Novacelli was wriggling like a puppy as he dropped to his knees beside the mattress, shrugging off his jacket. As it fell to the floor, he reached for Billy. Billy smiled as the maniac stroked his hair, inviting him closer.

"Hang on a sec," the drug dealer said as he sprang to his feet and walked quickly to the workbench.

Billy tested the strength of the clamp and tried not to imagine what the nutcase was rummaging for. Novacelli was back in no time with a pair of heavy-duty shears. Billy's eyes fastened on the big black and silver scissors in fascinated dread.

"What are those for, Rafe?" he couldn't help asking.

"A little fetish of mine," Novacelli said shyly.

Billy's heartbeat increased as Novacelli took down Billy's pants to reveal a pair of red briefs. Unconsciously licking his lips, the kidnapper plucked a fold of the soft fabric between thumb and forefinger. Pulling the cloth up in a tent, he cut a circle in the undergarment. Reaching through the hole, he pulled out Billy's balls and limp cock.

"Perfect," Novacelli said. "You're even wearing my favorite color. Hold real still for a few minutes, okay? I wanna look at you."

Novacelli sat as though entranced, his eyes fixed on the tableau of Billy stretched out on his back with his genitals offered up like some exotic dessert. As Billy's captor stared, a string of drool formed at the corner of his mouth and ran down to hang unheeded from his chin. Lying as still as possible, Billy tried to do nothing that would break Novacelli's reverie. As long as the little creep kept his hands to himself, he was welcome to look all he wanted. With luck, he would still be in a trance when Gareth arrived; and that Gareth would arrive, Billy had no doubt. Gareth Carey would not tolerate anyone taking what belonged to him. He would descend upon this place like a Category 5 storm, wreaking devastation on everything in his path.

Billy just had to stay alive until then.

# ~ Chapter Eleven ~

GARETH went to the closet behind his desk and came back with two wickedly small automatic weapons. Tossing one to Rick, the crime boss stuffed the pockets of his seven-thousand-dollar suit with clips.

"Do I get a toy?" Geordie asked.

"You're staying here," Gareth said.

"Why?" Geordie asked. "I should be the one going with you and…"

"And nothing, you dozy cunt!" Gareth roared abruptly. "This is an utter cock-up and the only person that I know I can trust is you. You have to hold the fort and wait for Paul."

"Fair enough, old son," Geordie said carefully. "I'll stay here and be your eyes and ears while you go get some old-school revenge. I know how it feels to want to pull the trigger yourself. Don't worry about things here; I'll handle Paul."

"Don't get too zealous," Gareth said, in a normal voice.

"I'll get the truth out of him," Geordie said grimly.

Gareth smacked Rick on the back. "Ready, mate?"

Rick turned his head to the side, audibly cracking his neck vertebrae. "Let's go get Billy," he said. He wasn't eager to go back to the scene of the bloodbath, but the thought of Billy in the hands of Rafael Novacelli formed ice crystals in his gut. Hefting the Kalashnikov, Rick shot a glance at Geordie and followed Gareth from the room. As they got into Gareth's car, it occurred to Rick that he hadn't had a chance to check in with his partner in far too long.

"What the flaming fuck are you waiting for?" Gareth barked.

Rick slammed the Quattroporte into gear. The big V8 engine roared as he maneuvered the Maserati sedan down the brick drive. With a scream of rubber on asphalt, Rick braked briefly at the street and then punched the accelerator. He glanced once at Gareth's pitiless profile, and kept his eyes on the road for the rest of the drive.

BILLY steeled himself as Novacelli leaned over him. He could feel hot breath on his cock and then wetness as his captor licked at him. The former rent-boy suppressed a shudder as the creep tongued every inch of skin exposed by the ruined underwear.

"You taste good," Novacelli mumbled. "You smell real good, too."

"I love taking baths," Billy replied, trying to suppress the nervous urge to babble and failing. "And I spend a lot of time in the pool. I guess I really like water. Weird, since I'm a fire sign. I should fear water, but I really love it."

"I could get you some," Novacelli said instantly.

"You'd do that for me?" Billy said. "Thank you, Rafe. I'd love some water."

"Okay. I'll be right back."

"I'll be right here," Billy said, rattling his chain and smiling to show he was kidding.

Novacelli laughed, a high-pitched sound that did nothing for Billy's nerves. As soon as his jailer left the room, Billy inspected the clamp his chain was clipped to. It was U-shaped to fit over the duct and fastened to a two-by-four with wood screws. All Billy needed was something thin enough to fit the screw heads and enough time, and he could free himself. Spotting the kidnapper's jacket on the floor, Billy snagged it with his foot and dragged it onto the mattress. The garment had several pockets and each contained something that was no doubt precious to Rafe, but was no good to Billy. He stuffed a few of the items under the mattress, but he found nothing that would work on the screws.

"What sort of electronics geek are you?" Billy muttered to himself. "Not even one teensy-weensy Phillips head screwdriver?" He lifted his head and froze at the sound of the warehouse door rolling up. "Please don't let that be more of this psycho's friends," he prayed to whoever might be listening to sinners like him.

RICK saw Novacelli come out of the door of the warehouse office right in front of him at the same time that Gareth entered the hallway from the other end. There was no way the undercover cop could take a shot without risking Carey's safety. As he hesitated, he was sprayed with water when Gareth fired, exploding the plastic bottle in the drug dealer's hand. Rick dropped to the ground as Novacelli returned fire. The gun barked again in Gareth's hand, but the Kutter had thrown himself backward into the office. A second later, a burst of gunfire came out of the doorway.

"Shit," Rick muttered. "Hey, Gareth! You could've killed me, you asshole!"

"Sorry, mate. Saw the shot and took it," Gareth called back. "What do you reckon that little ratbag's thinking right about now, eh?"

"I wish I had a change of underwear?" Rick guessed.

Gareth laughed, a bubbly sound that raised the hair on Rick's nape.

"You were supposed to wait by the back door 'til I scouted the place," Rick reminded his boss. "Now do you see why?"

"Fuck it!" Gareth said. "Let's get him."

Rick sighed. "Novacelli!" he shouted. "We've got AKs. If you don't come out of there, we're going to shred that cracker box you're hiding in." There was no answer and Rick had a very strong, very bad feeling. "Get the fuck down," he screamed at Gareth as he dove for the nearest cover. A split second later, an explosion lit the interior of the office like a lightning strike and a tongue of flame shot out to blacken the opposite wall. Debris rained down, pattering on the threadbare carpet, as dark smoke began to pour from the ruined doorway. "Gareth?" Rick called. He heard coughing and then Gareth came toward him through the roiling smoke. Grabbing Rick's arm, the big man pulled him to his feet. Rick realized his hearing was impaired when Gareth's lips moved soundlessly. "Can't hear," Rick yelled over the ringing in his head.

Gareth nodded his understanding.

"We should be a little more careful," Rick said. "Novacelli could be driving us into a trap."

Gareth nodded again and slowed his pace. When they reached the open space of the storage area, Carey took off his jacket and waved it around the corner. When nothing happened, he beckoned to Rick, putting his hand on the side of the other man's neck. Looking into Rick's face, Gareth spoke slowly so Rick could read his lips. "Thanks for the warning back there."

Gareth's voice was muffled, but Rick's hearing was returning quickly. Glad the damage wasn't permanent, he answered. "Just doing my job, boss."

Gareth grinned as he slapped Rick's cheek. "Since that didn't work out so well," he said, "why don't we do it your way this time?"

"I like the way you think," Rick said. "I'll take these stairs; you check around down here. You want me to go over it again?"

Gareth's eyes glowed with adrenaline-fueled energy. "I think I got it," he said as he moved stealthily away along the wall. "Happy hunting."

"I GOTTA get outta here. I gotta get outta here," Novacelli chanted as he tore around his room grabbing random objects. Abruptly, the lunatic stopped and turned to stare at his prisoner. "What am I gonna do with you?" he said.

RICK risked a look into the room before melting back against the wall. Squeezing his eyes shut, he cleared his mind and then looked through the doorway again. Novacelli was still standing over the bed with a gun in one hand and a fistful of Billy's hair in the other. Billy was handcuffed and leashed with no hope of escaping the bullet. Ruthlessly stamping on his flaring emotions, Rick made a decision.

Without shouting a warning, the undercover cop swung his gun through the opening and fired. Novacelli yowled in pain as the large-caliber bullet punched a ragged hole in his hand. The Kutter's gun thudded onto the mattress beside Billy's shoulder as Rick took aim again. Novacelli dove for his workbench, but the round came nowhere near him. Instead, Rick's shot severed the chain that kept Billy tethered. The cop hit the ground and rolled behind a tall tool cabinet, as Billy twisted and dropped between the bed and the wall. Novacelli was out of sight now, but he could be tracked by the noise he made as he scuttled along the littered floor.

"Rafael Novacelli!" Rick called out. "Give it up, punk. You've lost your weapon and you have a bad gunshot wound. Come on out here, and I'll get you an ambulance."

"Billy!" Novacelli cried out.

"What is it, Rafe?" Billy answered, and Rick grimaced as the kid gave away his position.

"I thought you were gone," Novacelli said in patently relieved tones. "Man, I thought things were really messed up for a minute there. Just let me find my other guns and I'll get rid of this asshole so we can be alone again. Where the fuck is that Eagle? I know I set it down here somewhere."

Rick pushed the wheeled metal cabinet over to the pile of mattresses where Billy lay flat on the floor, fastening his trousers. The young man looked up at Rick and tried for a nonchalant smile.

"You weren't here in thirty minutes," he said. "I'm not paying for the pizza."

Rick's heart clenched. This was one brave kid. If they got out of this dilemma alive, Rick was going to make a point of getting to know Billy Red, or Rose, or Willem Rosen, or whatever the hell he wanted to call himself. If this beautiful wreckage was salvageable, Rick was willing to undertake the project.

"Then I guess a tip is out of the question," the cop said, holding out his hand.

Billy crawled to Rick and crouched behind the tool cabinet with him. "Where's Gareth?" he asked.

Rick was shocked by how much the question stung. "He's around," he answered. "You ready to get out of here?"

Billy nodded and the tool cabinet began rolling back toward the door.

"Billy?" Novacelli called. "Where are you? I need help finding a gun."

Rick glanced at Billy, who rolled his eyes.

"Completely 'round the bend," Billy said. "Mad as they come. Thanks for coming to get me, by the way."

"It's why I get the big bucks," Rick said.

"Billy!" Novacelli said plaintively. "Why are you hiding from me?"

"When I say run, you get out the door and don't look back," Rick told Billy. "Take this phone. The first number is my partner."

"Why don't you call for backup now?"

"That's an awfully good question," Rick said.

"Oh God," Billy said. "You're not supposed to be here, are you?"

"No, he's not," Novacelli said from far too close. "But I'm gonna fix that right now."

# ~ Chapter Twelve ~

"DROP your gun," Novacelli said.

Rick and Billy turned and looked up into the barrel of a police-issued revolver. Rick didn't bother asking how Novacelli had acquired the thirty-eight. He put his own weapon on the floor and slid it forward.

"How the hell did you get behind us?" Rick wanted to know. "I could hear you on the other side of the room."

"I learned to throw my voice when I was a kid," Novacelli said. "My mom didn't like it one bit. It really freaked her out."

"You're so clever!" Billy exclaimed brightly as he rose to his feet. "But what took you so long to rescue me?"

Novacelli frowned in perplexity. "You were going to go with him," he said.

"Well, of course I had to pretend I wanted to go," Billy said.

"You were pretending?" Novacelli asked slowly.

"Of course." Billy's eyes were luminous with innocence. "Have you forgotten that we're soul mates, Rafe?"

Novacelli shook his head. "I didn't forget. Come over here by me."

Billy did as he was told, looking neutrally down at Rick. Rick didn't blame the kid for seeing the angle and playing it. It was the smart move. However, Billy ruined it when Novacelli aimed his gun at Rick's forehead.

"I'm not telling you what to do," Billy said. "But do you really want to kill a cop? That's right; he's a cop, and you know how cops are, Rafe. Kill a citizen and they'll come after you. Kill one of their own and they'll hound you to the ends of the earth and nail you into your coffin facedown. And then they'll kill you."

"But I need to kill him," the Kutter said sullenly.

Billy put a hand on Novacelli's cheek and turned the psycho's head toward him. "Look at me, Rafe," he said, his voice taking on a seductive purr. "You don't need to kill this man. Let's tie him up and get out of here. Let's go someplace nice where we can be alone together."

"I don't know," Novacelli said. "I don't know what to do. My hand hurts so bad I can't think right."

"You'd never kill a cop," Billy said. "You're too smart. You're smarter than all of them and I know it. And you know something else? There's nothing sexier than intelligence."

"You think I'm sexy?" Novacelli's eyes were locked on Billy's earnest face.

"I want you so bad right now," Billy said. "Come on; let's get out of here."

Novacelli swallowed hard, the sound audible in the stillness, and reached for Billy with his uninjured hand. Rick's fingers walked closer and closer to the stock of the AK-47 as Billy distracted the creep. Another few centimeters and Rick would have his weapon in hand, and Novacelli under arrest. And this long nightmare would almost be over.

GARETH nudged Epiphano's body with the toe of his boot, and then turned his gaze on Levere's lifeless face. A great sense of loss pervaded Gareth. Finding two more soldiers the size and temperament of Epiphano and Levere wasn't going to be a walk in the park. Guys like this didn't stroll up to you every day the way Rick had.

He dragged his eyes from the bloody corpses of his soldiers. As he looked around the warehouse at the bodies of the gang members, his emptiness was replaced by irrational rage at them for not being alive so that he could kill them. It was with the greatest effort of will that Gareth kept his finger from depressing the AK's trigger and shredding the remains of the Kutters into red rags. Teeth clenched in a parody of a grin, he started up the stairs.

"WHY hasn't Officer Miles called in?" Inspector Campbell Frehley asked.

"I assume he's busy," Graciela said a bit more sharply than she'd intended.

Graciela wished the inspector would just shut up about Rick not calling. She was worried enough as it was. Rick might be a cowboy, but he wouldn't leave her hanging like this without a good reason. And it didn't help that this bone-dry Brit kept reminding her every five minutes. Added to that, she was sitting at her captain's desk, which held none of her vast collection of stress-relieving widgets. Though Walter had given his office to Frehley for the duration, Graciela was afraid to touch anything. When this was over, Frehley would go back to Merrie Olde England, but she would still have to work with the captain every day.

"It's most frustrating," Frehley said from somewhere behind Graciela, "to finally have a chance to make contact with our man without compromising him, and then to lose it again immediately. I can feel my nerves fraying."

"And I can hear them," Graciela muttered.

Campbell Frehley stopped pacing and came to sit in a chair across from the desk. "Shall we talk about something else?" he asked. "Try and take our minds from it?"

"I don't think it's possible, but I'm willing to give it a try," she answered.

"What sort of man is Detective Miles?" Campbell asked.

"He's a good cop," Graciela said firmly. "He's smart, and not just book smart. He can't be rattled, and he can't be bought. I'd put my life on the line for him."

Frehley nodded. "All right. But I asked what sort of man he was."

"I told you. Rick's a cop, plain and simple."

"Really," Campbell relaxed a bit more in his chair. "And what does that mean to you?"

Graciela thought for a moment before she spoke again. "He can't see injustice without wanting to make it right, whatever the cost to himself. That's who he is, and that's why he became an officer of the law."

"He sounds exemplary."

"He is. I know what that word means."

"I wouldn't have used it if I didn't think you knew what it meant," Frehley said in mild reproof. "Not everything I say is an attempt to belittle you."

"Sorry. I'm a little touchy."

Campbell raised an eyebrow. "You're joking," he said dryly.

Graciela smiled despite her mood. "Okay, I deserved that."

"Tell me something, Gracie. Why are two such sterling members of your department forced to work outside of it?"

"I guess when you get right down to it, we wanted to prove we were just as good as the rest of the cops on the force."

"I would say that fact is self-evident."

"Yeah, and if promotion was based on merit alone, me and Rick might have better careers."

"So what is your fatal flaw?"

"Isn't it obvious that I'm Latina?"

"I would think that in today's politically correct climate you would be promoted automatically," Frehley said.

"Maybe. You're pretty shrewd, aren't you, *hombre*? Okay, it's true I've been offered a few things, but promotion comes at a price, and I can't pay it."

"What's the price, if it's any of my business?"

"They want me to rat out my partner so they can kick him off the force."

Campbell's eyebrows rose toward his widow's peak. "The perfect cop has a dark secret?"

"Yeah, and it's his secret, so don't ask me."

"I don't have to. I'm shrewd, remember?"

"I won't talk about it."

"Fair enough," Campbell nodded. "Why are you single?"

"*Que barbaridad!* Who do you think you are? My mother?"

"No. Just an interested unattached male."

Graciela's mouth dropped open and Frehley's phone rang simultaneously.

BILLY finished tying Rick's wrists together behind his back, leaning close to whisper in the man's ear. "Sorry. I did my best to keep them loose, but Rafe's got the peripheral vision of an owl."

"Not your fault," Rick murmured. "Keep him sweet if you can. Gareth will show up soon."

"Now there's a scary thought," Billy said. "Look, if anything happens…"

"Shhh. Nothing's going to happen to you," Rick whispered fiercely. "We're both going to live, because I have to tell you how I feel about you and you have to hear it. Okay?"

Billy's fingers tightened briefly on Rick's forearm. "Got it," he said and rose to his feet.

"I'm ready," Billy called to Novacelli.

Novacelli looked up from scrabbling around his workbench and his eyes widened as they focused on a spot over Billy's left shoulder.

"You're always ready, tiger kitten," Gareth said from the doorway.

PAUL MACROSS finished his call, dropped his phone in his pocket, punched his entry code on the security keypad and waited. After a few moments, he heard the thunks of the locks disengaging. The thick door swung open to reveal Geordie waiting in the foyer.

"Well, well. Been in the wars, Paulie?" Cook indicated Macross's bandages.

Paul narrowed his eyes at Geordie's jocular tone. "One of the bullets shattered my right ulna," he said, pointing to his cast and sling. "It's fucking painful. If I were you, I wouldn't fuck with me just now."

"Didn't the doc give you anything for that?"

Paul fished a bottle from his suit jacket and tossed it left-handed to Geordie. Geordie read the label and whistled soundlessly.

"Have a couple," the big man said as he twisted off the cap.

"Hell no, mate! That's codeine, just a step down from morphine. I'm not putting that shite in my body. That's for the losers we sell to."

"You have a point," Geordie said. "Come on in."

As Macross passed him, Geordie grasped the other man by his injured arm. Paul grimaced in agony and went to one knee.

"I have no sympathy for you; you could have taken the pills," Geordie said. "Now…I have one question for you, Paul. When you've answered it, I'll let go. Are you planning to fuck Gareth?"

"What?" Paul yelped in pain and consternation.

"Are you a filthy narc, Paul?"

"God, no!" Macross screamed as Geordie put an ounce more pressure on his arm.

"Are you quite sure?"

"Fuck yes, I'm fucking sure, you fucking bastard!"

"All right then," Geordie said, letting go of Paul.

Macross sat heavily on the marble floor, sweat beading his brow, cradling his injured arm to his chest. His panting breaths echoed loudly in the foyer, louder than Geordie's footsteps as he walked around Paul to squat in front of him.

"If you're not working with the Kutters, then you're simply a fuckwit," Geordie said dispassionately. "If it were up to me, I'd fire you permanently, but Gareth likes you. Therefore, you are being given a second chance. Here."

Paul set his jaw as Geordie tried to push a tablet into his mouth.

"Take it," Geordie ordered. "Just one to take the edge off. Don't worry; I need you sharp and wide awake. Sorry about the arm-twisting, but I had to know."

"No hard feelings," Macross managed to gasp.

Geordie put the pill on Paul's tongue and helped the other man to his feet. Macross swallowed, nearly gagging, but managed to get the tablet down. By then, Geordie had brought them to Gareth's office.

"What's going on?" Paul asked, leaning heavily on the mini-bar, holding a bottle of water awkwardly between his elbow and his side as he opened it with one hand.

Geordie looked up from rifling through the drawers. "You'll see," he said. "For now, you'd be smart to keep your mouth shut and do as you're told."

Macross nodded and waited for the dizziness to pass. His head had been spinning since that Lincoln had sideswiped them. He didn't think he'd ever forget the look on Billy's face as the young man was yanked into the big car. Paul had failed in his charge and he hadn't dealt with that yet. With any luck, the pain would keep the guilt at bay until he could handle it. For now, he'd be prudent and follow orders.

# ~ Chapter Thirteen ~

"HELLO, kids," Gareth said, stepping into Novacelli's room. "Can I play?"

"You can't have him!" Novacelli yelled at Gareth.

"Who the hell do you reckon you are?" Gareth asked coldly. "Look at you in your two-hundred-dollar sneakers and your trendy hair-don't. I'll wager your parents still carry you on their medical insurance. You're not a gangster, mate; you're just a misfit who's never had to work a day in his life. If you had come up from my streets, you might have a prayer of taking me, but the fact is that you're soft and I'm very, very hard."

"Nothing's ever good enough for you!" Novacelli shouted, apropos of nothing.

"And you're a shite-brained lunatic who's long overdue for a lesson about touching things that don't belong to you."

"Fuck you," Novacelli said.

"Fuck me?" Gareth replied. "Oh, no, no, puppy. Fuck you."

Gareth's automatic chattered and a stream of bullets flew toward Novacelli like chop from a fiberglass gun. Novacelli fired as he flew backward, but his shot went over Gareth's head. The junior gangster's body struck the workbench and dropped to the floor. After a few twitches, he lay still amid the dross of fast-food bags, plastic bottles, and cigarette butts.

"Well?" Gareth said, turning to a blood-spattered Billy. "Am I not your hero?"

Billy blinked and wrenched his gaze from Novacelli's corpse. "I suppose you are," he said.

"And?"

"And I shall be properly grateful when time and place shall serve," Billy answered.

"I see a mattress right over there," Gareth hinted.

"Jesus," Billy said, sleeving warm blood from his face. "Not here, please."

"Please?" Gareth repeated. "I was joking, but I like the sound of that word on your lips. Now where is Rick, my red angel?"

"Tied up behind that cabinet."

"Oh, good. That will save some time and aggravation. Not sure I could take him in a fair fight, but tied up suits me fine."

"What are you talking about?" Billy asked.

"Didn't you just tell Novacelli that our big blond stud is a copper?"

"Well, yeah, but only so Novacelli wouldn't kill him."

"What do you care if a psycho takes out a soldier?"

"He's a human being, Gareth," Billy said wearily. "That's all."

"Hello, Rick," Gareth said, pointing his weapon at Rick's head. "I feel bad about this, sport, I really do. I like you."

"Afraid I can't say the same," Rick answered.

Gareth smiled. "That's my boy," he said. "A smartass to the end."

"Wait!" Billy said. "Gareth, I want to make a deal with you."

Gareth chuckled. "What do you have that I didn't buy for you, crumpet?"

"How about your beloved product?" Billy said.

Gareth spun to point his gun at Billy. "If you know where it is, you'd better tell me right fucking now, kitten."

It was Billy's turn to laugh. "You know I'm not afraid of you, Gareth. You can hurt me, or kill me, but you can't make me do anything."

"That's true," Gareth said. "You sexy bitch, you. God, you make me harder than petrified wood. Would you consider blowing me for old times' sake?"

"Of all the stupid things you could do right now, putting your cock in my mouth would be the most stupid of all," Billy answered. "Do you want to hear the deal, or not?"

"Speak."

"I tell you where the drugs are and you leave here alone without looking back. Those are my terms. They are final and absolutely non-negotiable."

"Ooh, you make my balls tight when you go all cold and proper like that," Gareth said. "I just want to throw you to the ground and pry your legs apart and ram my…"

"Let's not get sidetracked reminiscing about the good times," Billy interrupted. "The cops are probably on their way, if they aren't outside already."

"Are you kidding? In this district? The cops will be here when the smell gets bad."

"You're too clever for me, Gareth," Billy said. "Do you want your drugs? Or is it worth more to you to continue tormenting me?"

"It's a harder decision than you might imagine, darling," Gareth said. "I suppose you want Rick's life as part of this bargain."

"I don't want anyone else to get killed," Billy said.

Gareth looked down at Rick. "Are you shagging him yet?" Gareth asked. "He's good. Puts up a real fight. Makes you work for it, but that's the best, isn't it?"

"You're sick," Rick answered succinctly.

"Oh yes, of course I'm sick," Gareth nodded. "But what about sweet, sweet Billy here? Why aren't you calling him sick? Why do people automatically side with the perceived victim? It's quite shortsighted of you, you know."

"I trust my feelings," Rick said. "Your failing is that you don't have any."

"That's my strength," Gareth disagreed. "But I've no time to debate the issue. Billy?"

"Do I have your word?" Billy asked.

"Of course."

"Look at me, Gareth," Billy said. "Do I have your word you'll leave here without killing Rick or me? Swear it."

Gareth pursed his lips, his gaze swinging between Rick and Billy. At last, he let the muzzle of the automatic weapon drop. "I swear," he said flatly. "Now tell me."

Billy pulled a set of keys from his pocket and tossed them to Gareth. "There's a black Yank tank parked in the east alleyway. It belonged to the late unlamented Rafael Novacelli and the enormous trunk is full of narcotics. There are more cached in the headliner, the door panels, and anywhere else you can think of that it would fit. Take it and bad luck to you."

"You really hate me," Gareth stated.

"With all my ruined heart," Billy said.

"You've no idea how badly I want to nail you at this moment," Gareth said.

"Nor do I care."

"Maybe we'll meet again," Gareth said from the doorway.

"If we do, remember to duck," Billy advised him, as he knelt to untie Rick.

Gareth's chuckle faded down the hall as Billy fumbled with knots that he'd tied such a short time ago.

"Hurry," Rick said. "He's getting away."

"That's the deal," Billy said.

"I didn't make any deals," Rick said, as the unmistakable sound of a large engine rumbling to life echoed dully off the side of the building. "Get a knife or something."

"I don't want to risk cutting you."

"God damn it, Billy! Just find something sharp."

In spite of Rick's urging and curses, Billy took his time loosening the ropes enough for the undercover cop to pull his hands free. Rick swept up his gun as they heard the sound of another vehicle arriving.

"Shit!" Rick said. "Give me my phone."

Billy tossed Rick his phone as he pulled something else from his pocket.

"Where did you get those keys anyway?" Rick said as he punched speed dial.

"Out of Novacelli's pocket; where do you think?" Billy said, as he pressed a button on the tiny box he held.

Rick's next words were drowned out by the sound of a massive explosion.

"FORGET it," Paul said. "I won't go along with this."

Geordie sighed as he closed the trunk of the BMW sedan parked in the drive of Gareth Carey's mansion. "Do you think Gareth feels the least bit of loyalty to you?" he asked.

"Doesn't matter. I took his money and I'm not going to cross him."

"Suit yourself," Geordie said, as he pulled his gun. "I've got everything from the safe and soon I'll have all the drugs, if that little weasel Novacelli hasn't gone completely insane and used them as fertilizer or something."

"You set all this up just to get the drugs?" Macross said incredulously.

Geordie smiled. "You want to change your mind? I could use you."

"Yeah. All right, mate," Paul said slowly. "That's a bit too tasty to pass up."

"Come on then. You drive."

Paul steered the BMW according to Geordie's directions and pulled carefully into the narrow alley beside the Kutters' warehouse. At the end of the lane was Novacelli's black Lincoln Continental.

"Park here," Geordie said as a door opened in the side of the gang's clubhouse.

"It's Gareth!" Paul exclaimed unnecessarily as Carey ran out of the warehouse and hopped into the Lincoln.

Something struck the side of Paul's head and he fell sideways, unconscious before he hit the door. A few minutes later, the burning debris from the obliterated Lincoln thumped on the hood and roof of the BMW, but Paul didn't stir.

"SO who was that on the phone?" Graciela asked.

"That was Paul Macross, my man on the inside," Campbell said. "It seems getting shot was enough to convince him to surface."

"And?"

"It's all falling apart. Paul's certain Hairy Carey is out for blood. Do you feel up to a field trip?"

Graciela got to her feet, patting her sidearm. "Got my permission slip right here," she said.

Inspector Frehley spoke into his radio as he walked from the office. Graciela followed, walking fast to keep up with the man's long-legged stride. In the lobby, they were met by some of Campbell's team members and hustled out to an armored van.

Graciela looked at the young men seated on two benches in the back of the van and a grin lit her face. "Looks almost like a SWAT unit," she said.

"It's awfully close," the inspector said, taking the wheel. "Have a seat."

Graciela slid into the passenger seat and belted herself in. "I assume we're headed for the Kutters' clubhouse?"

"You assume correctly. I hope we arrive in time to do some good."

Graciela nodded her vehement seconding of that notion and hung on as Frehley proved that he was much more than a desk jockey. She also clung to her fervent hope that Rick hadn't phoned at the agreed-upon time because he was too busy staying alive, and not because he was already dead.

# ~ Chapter Fourteen ~

RICK turned to stare at Billy as the remote hit the concrete floor with a flat cracking sound. The cop's eyes went to the device and then back up to Billy's face.

"You killed him," Rick said in dawning comprehension.

"Yeah, but it's not nearly as satisfying as I thought it would be," Billy said.

Rick blinked away sudden tears. This was the person he'd considered letting into his heart? This cold-blooded siren capable of playing hard men like Gareth and Geordie, psychos like Novacelli, and even hot-shit undercover cops? Why had Rick let himself even begin to believe that Billy was anything other than what he appeared? The young man's fathomless gaze focused on Rick as Rick leveled a gun at him. Billy held his arms out from his sides, hands open, took a deep breath, and waited to hear his fate.

"You're under arrest," Rick said. "You have the right to remain silent. You have the right to an…"

"I understand my rights as you have explained them to me, officer," Billy interrupted. "Now that I've been Mirandized, can I sit? I don't think my legs are going to hold me for much longer."

"Get on the ground," Rick said dispassionately, as the side door flew open.

Paul Macross put his hands up when Rick pointed his weapon. "Easy, mate," Paul said. "You can see I'm incapacitated, and I'm on your side anyway."

"What does that mean?" Rick asked.

"I can't show you my badge because I'm working covertly, just like you, but my superior will be here in a matter of minutes. So, if you could refrain from killing me until then, he'll show you all the badges you like and tell you that I'm a narcotics agent from Great Britain. Your DEA knows all about us."

"Can I call you butter, since you're on a roll?" Rick asked, feeling a little punchy. "Did you know I was a cop?"

Paul shook his head. "Not until I called in about twenty minutes ago. I came here with Geordie, but he knocked me out and I woke just now. There's a hell of a mess in the alley, by the way. I guess Gareth won't be standing trial after all."

"Where's Geordie?" Rick asked.

"After he cold-cocked me, I have no idea what happened to him."

"Maybe forensics will find two for the price of one," Rick said.

"We can hope," Macross answered as tires screeched on asphalt out in the street. "Can I let them in?" he added.

"Go ahead," Rick said, keeping his weapon trained on Paul.

Macross opened one of the roll-up doors and held his hands above his head. In a few moments, the warehouse was full of British and American officers searching it from top to bottom. Graciela spotted Rick and pushed past Frehley.

*"Esta milagro,"* she said. "How you doin', *hombre*?"

Rick finally let down his guard and hugged his partner fiercely. Over her shoulder, he could see Billy being handcuffed and marched toward the door. "Hey!" he called out. "That's my collar."

Campbell Frehley looked over from his conversation with Paul. "Understood, Detective Miles. We'll just take him into custody for now, if that suits?"

"Thanks," Rick said, leaning wearily on Graciela. "God damn, I'm tired, Gracie."

"Come on, *mi hermano*," she said, putting an arm around his waist. "Let's let the EMTs do their thing, and I'll take you home."

"I'm not hurt," Rick said.

Graciela looked as though she wanted to disagree with him, but she held her tongue. With a glance at Frehley, Graciela helped her partner outside and commandeered a cruiser. In a few minutes, they were tooling along in the relative peace of the patrol car's cabin. Rick let his head fall back and closed his eyes. He didn't remember ever feeling this exhausted in his life.

Graciela glanced aside at her partner's handsome profile. "Tell me," she invited.

"Not yet," he said without opening his eyes.

Graciela insisted on helping Rick into his apartment and into bed. When she was sure that he was asleep, she checked in with headquarters. After a few words with her captain, Graciela was passed to Inspector Frehley. "Rick seems okay," she said in answer to the Englishman's question. "A little strung out, but what do you expect after what we saw in that warehouse?" She listened for a few minutes and replied. "Yeah, I'm sure Rick will want to do the interrogation. Let us know when you're through with booking pretty boy. I'm going to hang here for now." Graciela's eyes drifted to Rick's bedroom door as she listened to Frehley. "Yeah," she said. "He just needs a few hours of sleep and he'll be ready; you can bet on it. Thanks, by the way. This could've gone a lot differently. See you soon, *cabron*. What?" She laughed softly. "I'll tell you what it means when I see you, if you haven't figured it out by then."

Snapping her phone shut, Graciela tapped it absently against her cheek. It was finally over and Rick was alive and unscathed, at least to the naked eye. She could see that something had happened to rock the foundations of Rick's world, but the bad guys were dead, or under arrest, and they could go back to their normal lives now. Rick could go back to normal. Graciela pushed away the thought that his normal life hadn't been all that happy and went to see what he had in the fridge.

"YOU ready for this?" Graciela asked as she and Rick got out of the car at headquarters.

"Don't insult me, Gracie," he said. "I wouldn't be here if I wasn't capable of doing my job."

"Okay," she said. "Willem Rosen is already in the interrogation room. Blake and McCray prepped him."

Rick made a face. "The *GQ* Twins," he said.

"Come on, *hombre*," she said. "They probably lulled Billy into a false sense of security with their sheer blondness."

Rick smiled faintly, gladdening Graciela's heart. "They must really be frosted that the case didn't get handed to them."

"Now you mention it, I think I detected a slight chill in their demeanor," she answered as they entered the hall that led to the interrogation rooms.

Blake and McCray were cool and professional as they congratulated Cruz and Miles on the collar, but it was obvious that they couldn't wait to leave. They were used to heading investigations and it chafed them to play a secondary role to Beanie and Weenie. Rick and Graciela tried their best not to gloat as the other two detectives briefed them. As Blake and McCray walked briskly away, Campbell Frehley and Paul Macross approached.

"I'm pleased to know you," Frehley said when he'd been properly introduced to Rick. "From what I understand it was your cool-headedness that kept the body count from being even higher. Good show."

"Thanks," Rick said. "That means a lot to me."

"Well-deserved," Frehley assured him. "I'm on my way to another meeting with your superiors. Be sure I shall speak highly of you and your partner. I just wanted the chance to shake your hand and tell you that I admire you."

Rick turned to watch Frehley walk away. "Your boss is a real class act," he said to Paul.

"He can be a right bastard when the occasion calls for it," Macross said. "Your forensics people are still working the crime scene, but it appears that the drugs did go up in the blast along with a very nice vintage Lincoln and Mr. Gareth Carey."

"Thanks to Mr. Willem Rosen," Rick said bitterly.

"Whoa, mate. You're making a mistake with this kid," Paul said. "He may be guilty of bad judgment, but he's a victim, not a perp."

Rick's eyes didn't soften at all. "I'm sure he's got a heartrending story, but he broke the law. I can't simply ignore that."

"Of course, you can. We make deals with killers all the time in exchange for testimony. Hell, we give some of them entirely new lives at the taxpayers' expense. Why not Billy?"

"Why Billy?" Rick countered.

"He took care of Hairy Carey for us," Paul tried a lighter tone.

"That's not funny to me," Rick said. "As far as I'm concerned, Billy Rose murdered Gareth Carey, and he'll stand trial for it. I promise you that young man will not escape justice."

"The two of you are the only ones that know what happened in that warehouse," Macross said. "At least hear his story before you send him to hell."

"He's going to prison," Rick corrected.

"For someone like Billy, what's the difference?" Paul asked.

Rick had a quick, but graphic, mental image of Billy held belly-down on a bunk by a muscle-bound convict with a shaven head and swastika tattoos while the neo-Nazi's buddies formed a line for the gangbang. "All right," he said. "If Billy wants to explain himself, I'll listen."

"Don't be too hard on him," Paul said. "That's all."

"I'll be fair," Rick answered. "That's all I can promise."

"That's all anyone can ask. I'm going to watch through the glass. You mind?"

"Why would I?"

"Just being courteous, officer. Why don't you join me later for dinner?"

"We'll see," Rick said.

"We'll see what?"

"If we still feel like eating after talking to Mr. Rosen."

# ~ Chapter Fifteen ~

RICK looked at the young man across the table. Despite the fact that Billy had been awake for more than thirty-six hours and had bruise-colored half-moons under his eyes, his appeal was still undeniable. Rick ruthlessly quashed the instinct to put his arms around the kid and crossed them over his chest as he sat back in his chair. "I'll ask you the same question I asked when I came to work for Carey. What were you really doing with him?"

"It was more convenient for me to whore for one man than for several clients," Billy said, his sweet voice tinged with acid.

"Why do you have to be a whore?" Rick asked neutrally.

"It's what you do when you find yourself on the streets."

"Why were you on the streets?" Rick was unrelenting. "You're healthy, intelligent, and certainly attractive; why do you have to sell yourself?"

"You want to know why I was on the streets? I hope you have a few minutes, because I have to start at the beginning."

"I don't care if you start with the day you were born," Rick said. "I just want the whole truth from you for once."

Billy gave Rick an odd smile and began to talk, sounding like a job interviewee giving an oral résumé. "The whole truth it is then. My father died when I was four. It turned out he'd never paid the life insurance premiums and we went from middle-class to poverty very fast. My mum cried a lot. She also drank a lot."

Rick's face was impassive. He'd heard too many stories that began much the same way.

"We were on the dole for a while and then Mum got lucky. She met a doctor in the spirits shop, and he asked if he could see her. They were married less than three months later. He bought her all the liquor she could hold, gave her Seconal like candy, and didn't demand much in the way of wifely chores. She thought he was a dream come true. He was my worst nightmare."

Rick had a good idea what he was about to hear and braced himself.

"My stepfather waited until I was twelve to start touching me," Billy said. "He didn't have actual sex with me until I was fifteen, but he made me touch him. He told me he'd divorce my mum if I said anything. I knew being poor again would kill her."

"So you kept quiet," Rick said.

"I didn't tell anyone," Billy confirmed. "I started doing badly at school. I got into fights. I disrespected everyone in authority. All the usual symptoms. My stepfather convinced my mother that I needed to see a therapist. The therapist they chose was a good friend of my stepfather's. They shared a lot of interests."

Despite his resolve to remain unmoved, Rick began to feel queasy.

"The therapist diagnosed me and prescribed a regimen of narcotics and weekly sessions," Billy continued. "This doctor would drug me, and then he and my stepfather would take turns banging me."

"That's sick!" Rick blurted out.

"Yeah," Billy agreed. "But wait; there's more. One afternoon, I was lying in a stupor on his couch with his cum drying on my face, and I heard him talking to my stepfather. Apparently, they belonged to some sort of organization of men like them. They were going to invite some of these men to a party where I was slated to be the entertainment. They were going to let these men shag me while they watched."

"And that's why you were on the streets?"

Billy nodded. "That was the last straw for me. The thought of all those strangers made me feel as crazy as they claimed I was, and, the next time I was alone, I ran. I had a little money, but it went away fast, and I couldn't think of anyone to call that wouldn't call my mum. The night finally came when I had to sleep on the street."

"Then you figured out no one would hire a runaway, but there was at least one way you could earn money, right?"

"The first time I sucked some bloke's cock in an alley..." Billy paused. "I felt so low. I couldn't imagine ever feeling lower, but I was still very young."

"How did you survive?"

"I was poaching on established territory, and I soon met the locals. Lucky for me, they were a lot softer-hearted than they wanted everyone to think. Mick, Scotty, and Ginger had an abandoned building they squatted in and they took me under their wing. There's safety in numbers, but you have to be alone sometimes and sometimes tricks go bad. I got knocked around and raped a couple of times, and then I got arrested."

Billy looked up, meeting Rick's eyes. "That was the worst. The cops put me in juvenile lockup with a bunch of skinheads that had been picked up earlier. The gang took turns shagging me until the lazy-arse guards came back to check on us in the morning. When I got out of hospital, my friends were waiting. They commiserated with me, took me home to the flat, and tucked me in and went right back out into the streets. I brooded for days. I knew I had to do something, or I'd end up dead before much longer. I grabbed my jacket and walked to where the lights were brighter. A car stopped and I got in. That's how I met Bevan."

"Bevan Barrow?"

"Yes, Bevan Barrow, the prominent London pimp."

"This isn't funny, Billy."

"Tell me something I don't know," Billy retorted. "Bevan took me home and got one of his women to clean me up. He told me over and over how beautiful I was, how fine, how I wasn't meant for the kind of animals that roamed the streets and that I deserved better. I soon found out what he meant by better. Better was me in one of the many flats he owned seeing customers by appointment. Better was the client giving the money directly to him. Better was him being able to avail himself of my services whenever he chose." Billy paused for a moment before he resumed speaking. "It wasn't long before Bevan realized he wasn't using me to full advantage. He put an end to my career as an ordinary whore and made me into something else. He sent me to live with what my grandfather probably would have called a kept woman. She taught me how to please a certain kind of man that lives outside the law, not just with sex, but other things. Bevan brought me home and used me as a reward. At first, if one of his men particularly pleased him, Bevan would give the thug a choice between a cash bonus and me. Later, like some Cockney sultan, Bevan would present me to visiting men of power that were so inclined. I went where he sent me and did who he told me to do. I didn't care anymore."

"Drugs," Rick guessed.

"Yeah. By this time, I was addicted to drugs. It started on the streets of course, but Bevan had access to anything you could name and was happy to provide me with whatever I wanted. I was using meth and coke to keep me going and morphine to let me sleep without dreams."

"I wish I could say I've never heard such a horrible story, but…"

"Yeah, I know; it's so cliché it's tiresome, isn't it? But why didn't I just walk away? That's what you really want to ask, isn't it?"

Rick nodded.

"Obviously, I stayed because that was where I belonged."

"That's not what Paul Macross says. He seems to think there's something worthwhile in you, though it's hard to tell what."

"I did get out of the life for a little while," Billy said softly.

"Well, don't stop there," Rick said. "Finish it. How did you go from gangster trophy fuck to this interrogation room with me?"

"It's kind of ironic," Billy said. "I met an undercover cop."

"And what happened?"

"Bevan gave me to Arthur for the night to impress him. Arthur tried to make a go of it. Even got as far as foreplay before he balked."

"And you were on to him."

"Yeah, but I didn't tell anyone. It seems to be a pattern of mine. The next time I saw Arthur, he was asleep in a chair beside my hospital bed. He'd saved my life. As luck would have it, his squad raided Bevan's place as I was trying to quietly snuff it in the bath. Arthur found me and called an ambulance. After all the excitement was over, he could've gone home, but he went to the hospital so I wouldn't be with complete strangers when I woke up."

"Sounds like quite a guy."

"Arthur Oldham was the best," Billy said firmly. "None better."

"What happened to him?"

"He met me." The young man crossed his arms on the table and put his head down.

"When you're through feeling sorry for yourself..." Rick began.

A hammering interrupted him. Rick called out and the door slammed open. Paul Macross came in and stood over Billy.

"You claim you knew Arthur Oldham?" the British cop said in a harsh voice.

Billy met the other man's eyes calmly. "You're not angry at me," he said. "You're angry with Arthur for not telling you."

"He told me he was taking a personal interest in a rehab," Paul said. "But I thought…"

"I'm not trying to dishonor Arthur's memory," Billy interrupted. "If you didn't know that he was…"

"What?" Paul interrupted, his tone daring Billy to say anything derogatory. "Arthur was what?"

"Gay," Billy said simply.

"Oh." Macross relaxed a trifle. "Of course I knew he was gay. Me and a handful of others. I knew Arthur could keep a secret, but he never said a word about you."

"Would you?" Billy said. "Of course not; you'd be just as ashamed of me."

"Arthur never did anything he'd be ashamed of," Paul said confidently. "If he didn't talk about you, it was for your protection, not because he was embarrassed."

"Thank you for saying that," Billy said. "Arthur…" His next words lodged in his throat. He couldn't get them out or swallow them down. Tears sprang to his eyes as he tried to breathe, but he felt as though he were strangling.

"You all right?" Rick asked. "You want some water or something?"

Billy shook his head, holding up one finger in a signal for time. After a moment, the spasm of intense sorrow passed, leaving the young man feeling drained and weary. "Sorry. Talking about Arthur affects me like this," he said weakly, as tears flowed unheeded down his cheeks.

"I'll tell Rick what happened," Macross volunteered.

Rick followed Paul into the hall and looked inquiringly at the other officer.

"I was part of Arthur's squad," Paul said. "I worked my arse off to get there; Oldham's Oldfellows had the best reputation of any narcotics team on the force. However, I hadn't been there long before Arthur was killed. When his cover was blown on the Carey case, he turned it over to another DCI. The Oldfellows were investigating a different dealer when Carey came out of hiding to kill Arthur. That's why Carey left England, just for the record."

"I'm sorry," Rick said. "The tone of your voice when you say his name tells me how much you admired him. Do you buy the kid's story?"

"It's certainly the kind of thing Arthur would do. It's hard for me to accept that he could have kept the relationship secret, but…"

"Do you think he…you know?" Rick let the implied question hang between them.

"Do I think Arthur fancied the lad? Of course he did. Don't you?"

"We're not talking about me," Rick said. "I'd like to hear more about Arthur Oldham, but right now, I want to finish the interview with Billy. I guess I will have dinner with you, after all. If the offer is still open."

Macross nodded and went back to the observation room. Billy looked up as Rick came back in and Rick wished that things were different. He clamped down on his emotions as he sat and continued the interview. "You were with Carey to get revenge," he baited.

Billy put his head back down and didn't answer. Rick crossed his arms and used the weapon that Paul Macross had put into his hands.

"So you've had experience with undercover cops," Rick said.

"I don't want to talk about Arthur anymore," Billy said.

"Then let's talk about me," Rick said. "When you realized I was a policeman, why didn't you tell me what you were doing with Carey? Didn't you think I would understand your need for justice?"

"You don't understand anything," Billy said. "When I had no place to go, Arthur took me into his home. He got me into a recovery program and I got clean. He took care of me through all of it. Most importantly, he didn't tell anyone, and I was able to get straight in peace. I can't begin to tell you everything he did for me."

"You fell in love with him," Rick stated.

"How could I help it? Arthur was big, blond, and handsome, so strong and yet so kind."

"How long were you lovers?"

Billy began to weep again and dashed his sleeve angrily across his eyes. "We were never lovers. He was too honorable to sleep with me. I asked. I begged. I even threatened, but he refused to take advantage of my situation, as he put it. Now he's dead, and I'll never know what it's like to make love with him."

"I'm...sorry," Rick said haltingly.

"Don't be. It doesn't matter," Billy said. "Nothing matters now."

"If nothing matters, why didn't you tell Carey I was a cop?"

Billy groaned. "You're going to make me say it, aren't you, you bastard? All right then; here it is. I didn't want anything to happen to you because I care about you. I don't want to care about you, but I do and there's nothing anyone can do about that, unfortunately."

"Why unfortunately?" Rick asked.

"Never satisfied, are you?" Billy answered.

"I just want the truth."

Billy sighed. "I couldn't let myself love another brave, honorable man just so I could watch him die," he said.

Several options passed through Rick's mind at lightning speed and he chose the one he thought would serve his purpose best. "You truly are arrogant," he said and was gratified when the young man looked up in shock. "Do you really think Arthur Oldham died because of you?"

"If Arthur hadn't taken me in, and let down his guard, Gareth wouldn't have been able to find him so easily," Billy said. "It's my fault that he's dead."

"Don't be so naïve," Rick continued. "And let's get back to the heart of the matter. You wanted to kill Gareth to avenge Arthur? Have I got that right? Then why don't you tell me what took you so long? You were alone with him plenty of times."

"I had to be sure," Billy said. "I had to know that he would die, not just be wounded. And I wanted to ruin him first."

"And you didn't want to get caught," Rick added.

"I didn't care about that," Billy said.

"Yes you did, or you would've taken a knife from the kitchen, or a gun from one of the bodyguards, and just killed Gareth while he was sleeping."

"I was working on the bodyguard gun angle," Billy said. "I was hoping to convince Levere that he had what it takes to bump off Gareth and run the empire, but he was a little less stupid than he looked. As for knives, I'll admit that I'm a coward. I couldn't stab anyone to death. I'm not even sure I could shoot someone. Pushing the button on the remote detonator was…disconnected, if that makes sense."

Rick pursed his lips and tilted his head to the side. "Your plan for Levere probably would have worked in time," he said. "Too bad I came along and screwed it up."

"Yes, you did," Billy said. "Although, I must say, Geordie was a worry and those Kutter boys threw a spanner in the works as well."

"You know what I think? I think you want to live."

"And I think you'll do your best to see that I don't."

Rick had no answer for that. He did intend to see that Billy was prosecuted for his crimes and if convicted, the kid could very well receive the maximum penalty. Abruptly, Rick stood and walked to the door without another word. He had nothing more to say; for him, the interrogation was over.

# ~ Chapter Sixteen ~

"SIT the hell down or dance with me," Graciela said as she set her mineral water back down on the bar.

Rick turned from his sentry watch on the door. "I wish the Brits would get here. I'm hungry enough to eat Mexican food."

"Eat me, you KY cowboy," she returned. Rick smiled at the familiar insult, but sobered quickly. Graciela noticed, of course. "When are you going to tell me what's eating you?" she asked.

"I don't think I can talk about it, Gracie."

*"Chingate!"* she swore. "What the hell happened to you, man? I know the scene in the warehouse got ugly. I can't imagine how you feel after you kill someone that looks like they should be in a schoolyard shootin' hoops."

"That was tough," Rick acknowledged. "Finding out the Kutters were responsible for Tonio's death took some of the sting out of it, though."

"*Que pasa*, man? I've never seen you like this and it bothers me."

"What am I like?"

"Dead," she said instantly. "It's like you died, but your body doesn't know it yet. You walk and talk, but…"

Rick turned on his barstool to look directly at his partner. "That's not a very pleasant thing to say, Officer Cruz. And what the hell does it mean?"

"You had this spark before you went undercover," she said. "I won't get this right, but I'll do my best. There was always this little gleam in your eyes, no matter what. A light that said to me that no matter what was happening on the outside, Rick was alive and well on the inside, doing his observing and pondering and…"

"Pondering?" Rick interrupted.

"Yeah, pondering, wiseass," Graciela repeated. "It's what you do. You watch and you think about things, and you always have this kind of humorous perspective even when it gets dire. No, not humorous. Yeah, humorous, but that's not exactly it. It's kinda Zenlike. *Ai, Dios mio,* I'm babbling. I told you I wouldn't be able to explain."

"You're doing fine," Rick said. "I guess I have lost my spark."

"Well, can you get it back? 'Cause it's like working with a zombie."

158

"Sorry," Rick said, as Paul Macross and Campbell Frehley entered the restaurant. "We'll have to continue this analysis later, doctor."

"You better believe it," she said, picking up her drink and following Rick to the table.

Graciela found herself seated next to Inspector Frehley and abruptly wished she'd worn something else. Her pants and shirt were appropriate for the setting, but a skirt would have given Frehley a chance to check out her legs. Reining in that line of thought, Graciela joined the conversation. "I'm glad Billy went for the deal," she said. "He doesn't seem all that bad."

"He's a killer," Rick disputed her opinion.

"He pushed a button," Paul shrugged. "A car filled with very good dope and a very bad man blew up and both are off the street. Try thinking of it like that."

Rick took a drink of his water instead of commenting.

"From Billy's testimony, I'd say the kid had plenty of reason to want Carey dead," Graciela filled in the silence.

Campbell nodded. "Carey was a nasty piece of work, all right. I shouldn't say this, but I'm relieved he won't be going to trial. If he didn't get convicted for some technical reason, I'm afraid I'd find myself looking at him through the scope of a high-powered rifle some fine day."

Graciela smiled at Frehley. Frehley smiled back, and Rick realized the other two were doing the cop version of flirting. He knew that at some point this evening, with the judicious application of alcohol, they would be competitively comparing scars, or something equally silly. *Good for you, Gracie,* he thought. *Wish I had your luck.*

"We'll walk back with you," Paul said, as Campbell settled the bill for dinner and Graciela headed off to the ladies' room.

"Not necessary," Rick said. "We can handle a simple prisoner transfer."

"No doubt," Paul said, "but it'll give my boss a little more time with your partner."

"They're grown-ups," Rick said. "They could just admit they're attracted to each other and want to spend time together."

"What world do you live in?" Paul asked. "Here on planet Earth we've worked out some rather elaborate masking mechanisms for our courtship rituals."

Rick smiled. "You're a funny guy, Paul," he said. "Is that a new thing? Because I don't remember you cracking wise when we were working for Carey."

"I was too bloody freaked out," Paul said. "I'm giving up undercover work. It's obvious I can't take the stress. My hat's off to you, though."

"Thanks, but I was plenty stressed, believe me. Especially after…" Rick paused. "Did I tell you that Billy knew I was a cop?"

"The whole time?"

"Almost from the beginning."

"And he said nothing," Paul marveled. "That lad really wanted to see Carey taken down. A pity you and he didn't join forces sooner."

"We didn't join forces," Rick said a bit more sharply than he'd intended.

Comprehension dawned in Paul's dark eyes as he stared at the other law officer. "You poor sod," he said softly.

"I'll be okay," Rick said, wishing this conversation were over.

"I can only hope to be as strong as you some day," Paul said. "I can't imagine having to arrest someone I love for murder."

"I don't love him," Rick said. "I thought I could, but I was wrong."

"Bullshit," Paul said. "You love him. And if you can watch him disappear from your life without blinking, you're a monster who's eaten his own heart."

Rick was relieved to see Frehley and Graciela coming across the room. Rick's partner looked at him curiously, as she joined them, but she didn't say anything until they were on the sidewalk.

"I told Frehley I'd show him the firing range," she said. "You think you and that proper Englishman can get our prisoner from the holding cell to the van?"

"Piece of pie," Paul said behind her.

"Cake," Rick corrected automatically.

"No time for dessert, mate," Paul replied.

"You two deserve each other," Graciela said. "Come on, Campbell. Let's go waste some ammo."

"Your partner's a major hottie," Paul said as he watched her walk away with Frehley.

"Yeah, I know," Rick answered. "And your boss has that 'I'm so uptight I must be a raging volcano in bed' thing down to an art."

"Couldn't testify to the volcano part," Paul replied.

The two detectives walked the three blocks to headquarters chatting about Graciela and Campbell. In a few minutes, they were down in lockup and Rick was signing papers for the duty sergeant. A short time later, an officer escorted a handcuffed Billy to the desk and turned him over to Rick.

"Miss me?" Billy asked brightly.

"Only because someone filed down the sight on my gun," Rick answered in kind.

Seeing the two of them together again, Paul knew his hunch was right. And not only did Rick Miles love Billy Rose, Billy loved him back. Suddenly, Paul's delicious dinner wasn't sitting so well, and he wished he didn't know what he knew.

"So how do you boys like my new look?" Billy asked, indicating his jail jumpsuit.

"Orange isn't really your color," Rick said.

"Bullshit," Paul joined in. "Every color is his color."

"Thanks," Billy said, and Paul saw how thin the lad's shell of bravado was.

"You'll be okay," Macross said. "They're putting you in maximum security for the night, but it's for your protection. Tomorrow, after the higher-ups fine-tune the deal, you'll be going to a safe house. Right, Rick?"

"It's true," Rick said to Billy. "The District Attorney's office, in its infinite wisdom, has decided that your testimony is so valuable that we're going to wink at the murder you committed. That's right, Billy. You won't be doing any time. In fact, you're going to be rewarded with a fresh start."

"Don't tell me I've won the lottery as well." Billy refused to be outdone in flippancy.

Rick's eyes narrowed at the corners, and Billy knew he'd scored a hit. "I wouldn't be surprised," the cop said. "In addition to the get out of jail free card, you'll be receiving a brand new name, and that's not all. The taxpayers are providing you with a new job, too. Of course, your old job skills probably won't be much use to you there, but the state couldn't find an opening for a drug lord's toy boy."

Billy clutched his chest dramatically. "You got me," he said melodramatically. "I shan't recover from that one."

Paul butted in on the sniping again. It was too painful for him to watch two people that should be hugging raking at each other with words. His mocking joke about human courtship rituals came back to haunt him. "Come on," he said. "The van's waiting and I don't want to be at this all night."

Rick nodded and they marched Billy down a long hall to the back of the building where they exited onto a small loading platform next to the Dumpsters. Beside the concrete platform, a large van idled with the rear doors already open.

"Hold on," Rick said, putting a hand on the butt of his weapon.

"What's wrong?" Paul asked.

"Where the hell is everybody?" Rick asked as the flat crack of a gunshot echoed off the wall.

Rick dove onto Billy, shielding his prisoner from the gunfire with his body. Paul was crouched in the doorway behind them, weapon in hand, searching frantically for the source of the sniper fire. Sharp chips and brick dust showered Rick's back as he pushed Billy ahead of him into the van. As Rick jumped from the platform, a round struck him in the leg, and he crash-landed in the vehicle's cargo bay. Billy broke Rick's fall, but the handcuffs prevented the young man from doing much else besides provide padding. Rick sat up, pointing his gun toward the back of the van, but the firing had ceased for the moment. Risking a look down, Rick saw that his wound could've been worse. "Macross!" he shouted. "You alive?"

"And kicking," Paul answered. "I think the shooter's on the move."

"Stay where you are," Rick ordered. Making a snap decision, he unlocked Billy's cuffs. "If you run," he said, "there will be nowhere in the world that you can hide from me. Understand?"

"I would never run from you," Billy said.

"Stop that," Rick said fiercely. "I know what you're doing, and I'm not going to fall for it again. You're good. You're really, really good, but I'm wise to you now."

"I know," Billy said. "I knew what I was giving up when I pushed that detonator button, but I had to do it. I promised Arthur Oldham's ghost that I'd get Gareth Carey for him."

"Shut. Up."

"We might die any second." Billy moved closer to Rick. "I'm not going to my grave without telling you that I love you and I would do anything if I thought I could change your mind about me."

Rick pointed his gun at the young man. "I'm warning you."

"Shoot me, then," Billy dared him. "It would be a mercy killing. My life is over anyway if you're not going to be in it."

"How could I ever believe a word that came out of your mouth?" Rick was goaded into saying. "You've made a career out of deception."

"And how is that so different from your job?"

"I'm not listening to you anymore," Rick said. "You'll make everything sound reasonable in that creamy voice, and then you'll befuddle me with that killer face and body and before my head stops spinning, you'll be somewhere like Acapulco with all the money and I'll be picking up the pieces."

"I understand that you don't trust me," Billy said. "I accept the consequences of my actions. However, nothing says I have to like it."

"You okay in there?" Paul yelled just as another round of gunfire began.

This time there were a lot more guns as the men in the building arrived in response to the first shots. Bullets began to hit the armored van and it was apparent where the sniper had taken up a new position.

"We're going to be taking fire soon," Rick said. "Get as far in the front as you can."

"Fuck that," Billy said and hopped over Rick.

"Stop!" Rick shouted as the kid put his hand on one of the back doors.

A bullet flew past Billy's cheek and slammed into an interior wall of the van. Rick threw himself at the young man, ignoring the pain of his wounded leg, as he grasped Billy's ankle.

"Wait," Billy said, as Rick began hauling him backward. Lunging forward, the young man managed to grip the inside handle of the left door and pulled it closed. Another round zinged into the vehicle through the open space on the right, narrowly missing Billy. Desperately, Rick yanked on the kid's leg, pulling him out of range as the other door slammed shut.

"Idiot!" Rick yelled. "You could've been killed."

"And you care because?" Billy's question took all the wind out of Rick's sails.

"You're so smart," Rick said. "Geordie told me that and damned if he wasn't right. What a waste." Billy's eyes glittered with tears and Rick steeled himself against their power. "Oh please," the cop said. "Not the waterworks, not you. Not the tough cookie that slept his way into Gareth Carey's bed with the express intention of killing him. You're just going to disillusion me if you cry."

"You took pity on me once before when I cried," Billy said. "I thought it was worth another try."

Rick looked intently at the young man wiping wetness from his cheeks, but it was impossible to tell if Billy was serious or not.

"You can come out now!" Paul yelled. "The sniper's gone." The van doors opened and Paul called over his shoulder. "Get an ambulance here; we have an injured officer."

"It's not mortal," Rick said quickly, as he sensed the tension in the air ratcheting up several notches. "Thanks for the assist, guys."

The police officers standing around the van with drawn guns began to disperse. The sound of a siren could already be heard as the EMTs approached. Paul took out his cuffs and started to put them on Billy.

"You don't have to bother with those," Rick said. "The prisoner promised me he wouldn't run."

Paul and Billy both looked at the wounded man as though he'd taken one in the head instead of the leg.

"Whatever you say," Paul shrugged, as the medics swarmed over Rick.

"Get your boss up here," Rick said from the center of a flurry of purposeful activity. Frowning in irritation, he beckoned Macross closer and spoke in the Brit's ear. "We need the inspector's influence to get Billy released to our custody so we can take him directly to a safe house. And no one else needs to know about it, okay?"

Paul nodded as he straightened up. "I'm assuming that this was a hit arranged by friends of the late Gareth Carey, yes?"

"You can bet whatever you like on that," Rick said. "I caught a glimpse of the sniper as I was diving for cover. It was Geordie Cook, big as life. You can tell forensics to stop sifting for him at the blast site."

"Geordie?" Billy said. "No. That isn't right. Geordie's the king of the pragmatists. He'd cut his losses and run back to the UK."

"You sound so sure," Paul said.

167

"Gareth felt a particular loyalty for Geordie and a few other blokes from his old neighborhood, but it bloody well wasn't reciprocal on Geordie's side," Billy said. "Geordie pretended he felt the same, but he was fucking Gareth in a very big way. Among other things Novacelli told me was the fact that Geordie and the extinct Kutters had their own deal going."

"Whatever his reasons," Rick said, "Geordie was on the roof across the lot with a rifle."

"And he can't shoot worth a tinker's damn," Billy observed. "You're the only one wounded and it isn't even life-threatening. Sorry, but it really isn't that bad for a gunshot wound. Don't you think it's odd that Geordie couldn't hit anyone else?"

"The lad's right," Paul said. "Unless Geordie really is that bad a shot."

"If he was, he would've sent someone else to do the job," Rick said. "Damn you, Billy. Why is everything about you so complicated? I should've shot you in the van when I had the chance."

"Easy, mate," Macross said.

"It's okay," Billy said. "It's his way of apologizing."

"No, it sure the hell is not," Rick said, as the EMTs finished up.

"Come on," the young man said. "Admit it. I'm not that bad."

"In the eyes of the law, you are," Rick disagreed.

"I don't care about the law," Billy answered. "It's your eyes that matter."

"I told you to stop that," Rick said. "I'm not letting my guard down just because I'm hurt."

"I didn't think you would." Billy walked away as Inspector Frehley arrived and beckoned to him.

# ~ Chapter Seventeen ~

"CAN he really do that?" Rick asked. "Can he request a particular officer to guard him?"

"Looks that way, *hermano*," Graciela said.

"I was there too, you know," Rick pointed out. "They could use my testimony."

"You don't have the kind of detailed info that the kid does," she reminded him. "Looks like Gareth paid off quite a number of elected officials to look the other way."

"I just don't see why we have to guard him."

"Why don't you quit complaining? I get to work with Campbell some more, and you get to lounge on a comfy couch with a heroic wound and have control of the remote all day. What more could a man want?"

Rick looked up at her from under his brows, as Billy entered from the kitchen.

"What is that incredible smell?" Graciela asked.

"Brownies," Billy said. "They'll be cool enough to eat in a minute. Why don't you have one? Or two?"

"Brownies? You are pure evil, *chico*," Graciela said. "There is no greater temptation in all existence. Of course, I should just apply them directly to my thighs and bypass the whole eating thing."

Billy scoffed at her. "Look at you; you're a rock. If you were in any better shape, people would mistake you for an aerobics instructor."

"Shut up!" Graciela said delightedly as she left for the kitchen.

"Why are people always saying that to me?" Billy mused.

"It's not going to work," Rick said for perhaps the twentieth time. "You can stop being all cute and domestic any time now."

"No, I'm afraid I can't," Billy said. "Since that's what I've decided to be in my new life. I thought you'd be pleased that I've turned over a leaf, as they say."

"It doesn't matter what I think," Rick said. "Do whatever you want."

A second later his arms were full of a warm, chocolate-scented body and a bold tongue was snaking past his lips. Rick put his hands on Billy's chest and pushed the young man away. "Okay," Rick said. "You get that one free because I chose my words carelessly. If you ever do that again, I'll smack you without thinking twice."

"Won't be the first time I've been smacked," Billy said. "Come on, Rick. You don't have to love me; just make love to me."

"There must be a language you understand 'no' in," Rick said. "I just have to find it."

"What's wrong with a little sex?" Billy wanted to know. "I'll even take it easy on you since you're wounded."

"Best offer you've had in a while," Graciela said from the doorway.

"Private discussion, Gracie," Rick said.

"I don't mind if you stay," Billy told her.

"God damn it!" Rick cried out in frustration. "I thought you said you were resigned to the fact that you lost any chance of being with me."

"I know you can't love me," Billy said. "And I'm going to vanish soon. If I'm ever going to have a chance to sleep with you, this is it."

"And that's important to you, is it?"

"Why else would I be making such a fool of myself?" Billy asked.

"Good point," Graciela said through a mouthful of brownie.

"Gracie," Rick said, and his partner retreated into the kitchen.

"Why do you want to fuck me so bad?" Rick asked with deliberate crudity.

"Well, first of all, you're hotter than the sun. I've never been so powerfully attracted to anyone. In a physical sense, I mean. I get hard if I hear your voice in the next room."

Rick raised his eyebrows.

"I'm not exaggerating," Billy said. "You have the most seductive voice I've ever heard."

"No one's ever told me that before."

In the American's vibrant baritone, Billy heard the echoes of Arthur's voice, and he put a figurative finger over the ghost's lips. Arthur was gone; the man that had haunted Billy's memories for nearly two years had not been miraculously resurrected when Gareth died. Somehow, the young man would have to start living with that fact. No way was he going to make the same mistakes with Rick.

Rick flinched back as the kid leaned over, but all Billy did was put another cushion under his bandaged leg. Not for any money would Rick admit it, but the ache lessened as soon as the limb was elevated. With a small frown, the detective watched Billy pick up his medication bottle from the end table.

"This is the same amount that was in here yesterday," the young man said.

"I didn't need any last night," Rick said.

"That's why you're gritting your teeth? Because you aren't in pain?"

"Leave me alone," Rick said.

"It's kind of hard to do that when we're living together."

"We're not living together. You're testifying for the prosecution and Graciela and I are guarding you in case Geordie decides to take another shot at offing you."

"It sounds so romantic the way you say it," Billy said.

"Go away, please. I'm trying to watch football."

"That's hockey."

"Do you have a point?"

Billy shook his head, grinning impishly.

"Gracie!" Rick called. "Come and get the kid, please."

"I'll go," Billy said. "Would you like a brownie?"

Rick struggled with himself for several moments before admitting defeat. "Yes, please," he said.

Graciela plopped down on the arm of the couch a few minutes later and handed Rick an enormous square of chocolaty, chewy, melt-in-the-mouth lusciousness and a glass of milk. "I can see how hard you're trying to hate the kid," Graciela said. "So maybe you'd better not eat that. I had one half that size and I want to bear his children."

Rick rolled his eyes and took a bite. "Delicious," he said grudgingly.

"Why don't you tell him?"

"You know why."

"Come on, Rick. I know that what he did was wrong, but he had some *raaaawther* compelling reasons, as Campbell would say. We're realists, *hermano*. We know there's no such thing as justice or a fairy-tale ending. But even if we can't live happily ever after, we are entitled to a little happiness occasionally. Why won't you allow yourself that?"

"With Billy?"

"Yeah, with Billy. Why not? He loves you and you love him. Doesn't happen every day."

"Why does everyone think I love him?"

"You watch him when you think no one's looking," she said. "The longing in your eyes, *ai Dios mio*, it breaks my heart."

"Sorry," Rick said.

"Asshole. The least you could do is throw him a bone. Go in the kitchen and tell him you like his brownies. And stop smirking, you gutter-brained rump wrangler."

"Hand me my crutches, woman," Rick said. "If it'll shut the both of you up, I'll hobble to the kitchen and have another brownie."

"You're a good man," Graciela said. "Want help?"

"I can make it. Here, guard this with your life."

Rick tossed Graciela the remote control and limped out of the den area. As he negotiated the doorway to the kitchen, Billy quickly turned his back and busied himself at the counter. His suspicions easily roused, the cop hastened forward, catching the rubber tip of one of his crutches on a chair leg. If Billy hadn't looked around at that moment, Rick would have taken a spill on the tiled floor. As the young man steadied him, the police officer saw the shine of dampness on the kid's cheeks. Rick almost let it go without comment, but found he couldn't. Annoyed by his weakness, he spoke brusquely. "What are you crying about now?"

Billy shook his head, his throat too tight to allow the passage of words.

"Cat got your tongue?" Rick asked. "Would it help if I told you that was the best damn brownie I've ever had?"

Fresh tears overflowed and ran down Billy's face. The young man grabbed a tea towel and furiously mopped the moisture away. "Sorry," he said. "I...I'm sorry."

Rick sighed as the kid broke down completely. "Sit," he said. "Tell me about it."

Billy dropped into the chair that had tripped Rick up. "I was th-thinking about A-Arthur," the young man stammered through his weeping. "He wuh-wouldn't be too puh-proud of me."

"No, I don't suppose he would," Rick said. "Not the guy Paul told me about, anyway. That guy wouldn't have condoned killing for any other reason than self-defense."

"I know," Billy sobbed. "What have I duh-done?"

Rick lowered himself into a chair next to Billy's. "You avenged your friend," he said. "But now you realize that you dedicated yourself to something unworthy, something your friend wouldn't approve of. You wish you could take it back, but that's not the way the world works."

"I killed someone and I can never make it right."

"Shhh," Rick said, putting a hand over Billy's. "You're right; you can't change it now, but you can make sure it doesn't happen again."

"Never," Billy vowed through his tears. "This is going to gnaw at me for the rest of my life."

"You're right about that, I'm afraid," Rick said. "It surely will. But it does get a little easier to bear after a while. A little."

"I wish…"

"What?"

"Forget it. You've turned me down in every way known to man."

"You really want me that much?"

Billy nodded. "Call me shameless, but if I can guilt you into it, or rouse your sympathy, I won't hesitate to use those methods. If I have to lose you, at least let me have one good memory to take with me."

Rick absently stroked the smooth skin of Billy's forearm as he thought about it. "All right," he said finally. "But let's be clear. This is not a sympathy fuck. I'm going to make love to you because I want to. You caused Gareth Carey's death, but I just can't make myself believe that you're evil at heart."

"I don't want to be a bad person." Billy's tears began to fall again.

"Hush, now," Rick soothed him. "You're not a bad person."

Arthur's words on Rick's lips nearly undid the young man, but he managed to speak. "How can you be sure?" he asked, as he'd not dared ask Arthur.

"Well… I'm a good person, right?"

Billy nodded his wholehearted agreement.

"Would I love a bad person?"

Billy shook his head.

"Then you must be one of the good ones, too."

There was complete silence in the kitchen for a long moment before Billy swallowed audibly and cleared his throat. "It's too much," he said. "I don't deserve your love. Just make love to me, and I can go into the program with something to hold onto when I'm feeling blue."

"I'll give you plenty to hold onto if you let me," Rick said. "Just a second. Let me finish. You really put me through the wringer. No; wait. It was more like a blender. I've loathed you, pitied you, lusted after you, deplored you, loved you, hated you…and now I love you again. I said let me finish. The truth is I started loving you the second you flounced up to Gareth's table and gave him a ration of shit, but I couldn't let myself feel that way about the perp's boyfriend no matter what my heart wanted."

"Finished?"

"Yeah, I guess. All I'm saying is that I loved you all along, but I couldn't, if that makes any sense at all."

"I'm afraid I'm going to start weeping again," Billy said.

"Come here."

Rick reached across the short space that separated them and pulled Billy into his arms. The young man returned the embrace, climbing onto Rick's lap facing him, resting his cheek on top of the other man's head. Rick ignored the doubts that bade him push Billy away, and hugged him tightly instead. Laying his head on Billy's chest, Rick listened to the racing heartbeat and tried not to think so much.

"I'd really like to kiss you," Billy murmured against the other man's jackstraw hair.

Rick offered his lips to Billy. The reformed rent-boy regressed, diving on the proffered lips as though the meter was running, using all his wiles to arouse the other man with this caress. It worked as well as ever with one significant and crucial refinement. Rick's response had the same kindling effect on Billy.

"Um, I'm truly sorry to have to say this," Rick drawled when their lips finally parted. "But could you get up?"

"Oh, your leg! Fuck! I'm sorry!" Billy gasped.

"No, it's not my leg," Rick said with a significant glance downward.

Billy's eyes fell to the swell at Rick's crotch. "You sure?" he quipped. "Because it felt like a leg to me."

"Clown."

"But I'm your clown," Billy said, cupping Rick's chin with his palm, looking into a stare hot enough to melt steel. "Can I have another kiss?"

"You can have pretty much everything you see," Rick answered.

"Does 'get a room' mean anything to you?" Gracie asked from the doorway.

"Jealous much?" Billy countered.

"Course not, gorgeous," she said. "Rick and I share everything. Hope it's not a problem with you if I join you two on occasion."

Billy's head spun around, and he fixed an incredulous stare on Rick.

"Oh, for cryin' out loud! Surely, you don't believe her," Rick yelped.

"I'm not taking any chances," Billy answered. "Come on; let's go somewhere more private. I've been fantasizing about this since the pool house."

Graciela raised an eyebrow. "Pool house?" she repeated with interest.

Rick took Billy's hand. "Can't talk now, Gracie," he said. "Gotta go."

Campbell Frehley entered the kitchen just as Rick and Billy were exiting down the hall that led to the bedrooms. "What are they doing?" he asked.

"Same thing we're gonna be doing, if I'm lucky," she winked broadly.

Graciela had the distinct pleasure of seeing Campbell look surprised for the first time since they'd met. Then the back of her thighs were against the kitchen table and the long, cool Brit was leaning over her with an arm around her waist.

"I trust I've not misunderstood you," Campbell said, just before their lips met.

"No misunderstanding, *hombre*," she said. "But I didn't mean right here and now. Geordie Cook is still out there somewhere and somebody in this house needs to stay alert."

"I'll radio Paul to bring in the chaps from the perimeter," Campbell said.

"Your eagerness is flattering, by the way," Graciela said. "Not to mention out of character, but I think we should cool it for now."

"You are wise," he bowed to her restraint. "However, I will confess to you, woman, that you stir me so that you make me forget my duty."

"Almost," she amended.

"Almost," he agreed. "Any rule against staying alert together?"

"Nope," Graciela said, kissing his cheek and reaching blindly for the platter on the table behind her. "Here. Have a brownie."

# ~ Chapter Eighteen ~

"THIS is weird," Billy said as he closed the bedroom door. "You've seen me naked before, but I feel...shy all of a sudden. Is that weird?"

Rick smiled, despite the turmoil of his feelings. "It's a little weird," he agreed. "Considering what an exhibitionist you pretended to be."

"Who was pretending?"

"I see that being a smartass wasn't an act either," Rick answered.

"Would you rather have a dumbass?"

"I think I'd like to have Willem Rosen, if he's home."

Billy met Rick's eyes. "How do you do that?" the young man said.

"What?" Rick put a hand on Billy's neck, stroking the hinge of the young man's jaw with his thumb.

"Remind me of who I really am."

"My partner was born with a bullshit detector and I think it rubbed off on me. Just be you, Billy. You don't have to hide from me."

"You're going to make me cry again," Billy said. "I've saved up a lot of tears in the last two years."

"You were with Carey for two years?" Rick asked in disbelief.

"Of course not," Billy said. "I would've killed myself by now. It's been almost two years since Arthur was…"

Rick put his arms around Billy and held him tenderly. "You talk too easily about killing yourself," Rick said. "Let's see if I can't convince you that life is a pretty good alternative."

"You're going to convince me with sex?" Billy raised his head from Rick's shoulder. "I don't want to rain on this particular parade, but sex is what I do. It's not much of a reason to get up every morning."

"Then you're doing it wrong," Rick smiled. "Sex can be a wonderful, joyous, bonding, life-affirming experience—providing you love the person you're doing it with."

"I've never had…" Billy's voice caught, and then he continued. "I've never… made love with someone that really cared about me," he said frankly.

When Rick heard these words, he knew without doubt that the snare had closed around him, and he would never be free of his love for this young man. Moreover, he knew that no matter what came of this union, he would not regret it because it was a chance at true love. Even if it was only one in a million, a long shot was better than no shot at all. "Why do you think I stayed at Gareth's after you told me you knew I was a cop?" Rick asked.

"You wanted to bust him."

"No. I stayed for you," Rick said, kissing Billy's forehead. "Because I care about you."

Billy shivered in anticipation. "Show me," he invited.

Rick tilted his head and took Billy's mouth in a long, slow, deep kiss that Billy was praying would never end. Lips and groins pressed firmly together, the two men moved dreamily against each other in the late evening gloom. Maintaining the sensual contact, Rick's nimble fingers danced down the front of Billy's shirt, unfastening buttons and sliding under cool cotton. Billy made a small sound into Rick's mouth when the exploring hands brushed his nipples.

"You taste so good," Rick said as he relinquished Billy's lips. "Sorry for the break in the action, but just so there are no misunderstandings: you want to make love, right? The whole enchilada?"

"I want your beautiful cock inside me," Billy said. "I've only held it in my hand so far."

"I think I can oblige you," Rick said. "Although the holding thing is nice too."

Billy didn't have a comeback to this banter. Rick stopped rubbing lightly at the young man's nipples and looked into his eyes.

"What is it?" Rick asked. "Is there something that bugs you that I should know about? Or some fantasy you have? Just tell me."

"I won't cum," Billy said.

"Excuse me?"

"I can't," Billy said. "Not while we're, you know.... Not while you're inside me."

"Sure you can."

"No, really. I can't."

"I'm betting you can," Rick said. "I just have to find your trigger, and I don't care how long it takes me."

"Don't make it a pride thing," Billy said.

"Pride's got nothing to do with it," Rick assured him. "When you cum, it'll be because you want to, because you love me. Now let's stop talking about it. What do you say?"

"Well, if you're determined to make me cum, I won't stand in your way," Billy said.

"That's my boy," Rick said, pushing the shirt from Billy's shoulders and down his arms.

Rick urged Billy to sit on the bed and settled beside him. With gentle, almost reverent touches, Rick accelerated the young man's breathing and heart rate. When Rick pushed against Billy's sternum with a fingertip, the kid lay back with a moan of pure desire.

"What?" Rick asked facetiously. "I didn't quite catch that. Could you repeat it?"

"Mmm, I said. Why don't you take your clothes off so I can feast my eyes on that splendid body and that enormous bum-tickler you carry around between your legs?"

Rick grinned. "Is this how you talked to your clients?"

Billy stiffened immediately and Rick lay down beside him. Stroking the young man's chest, Rick spoke gently, but firmly.

"We can't let our past be this thing we never talk about," the cop said. "If we give it that kind of power, it will eventually split us apart. I know what I'm talking about here."

"It's hard for me," Billy said.

"You bet it is," Rick said, pushing off his jeans.

Billy's eyes went to the other man's crotch, taking in the long cock, unfettered by boxers, briefs, or any other version of male undergarment. It was hard all right, hard and thick and curved perfectly to fit inside Billy. Billy was sure of it. "Okay," the ex-callboy said. "I'll make a bargain with you. I'll agree to talk about anything even if it cuts me to the bone. You agree to give me your willy whenever I want it."

Rick frowned. "I can't see a down side for me, but there has to be a catch to a deal this good."

Billy chuckled softly and Rick's erection twitched in anticipation. "Look at you," Billy said. "An hour ago, you hated me, and now you can't wait to top me."

"Actually, the two aren't mutually exclusive, but I told you, I never really hated you. I just…. I knew it wouldn't be a good idea to love you."

"You're probably right about that," Billy said as a naked Rick lay back down next to him.

"I don't care anymore," Rick said, touching the young man's cheek. "I want to love you and I want to believe that you love me. At the risk of repeating myself, I'm consciously making the decision to take this chance. Okay?"

"Still protecting the naughty boys?" Billy asked as Rick's fingers trailed down his neck.

"Yeah, but I'm narrowing my focus," Rick said, dipping his head to kiss a beckoning nipple.

"Only the naughtiest?" Billy guessed.

Rick's tongue circled the puckering nub, and then he drew it between his lips. A sigh of pleasure made the man smile around the resilient flesh he was sucking. Taking the nipple between his teeth, Rick basked in the quick intake of breath that emerged as a pleased groan and a request for more.

"Is this something you particularly like?" Rick asked. "Because I could do this all day."

"You bloody wonderful man," Billy said breathlessly. "Yes, I like it. I like it a lot."

"How about this?"

Rick deftly unfastened Billy's trousers and slipped a hand inside. Grasping the warm, suede-skinned length of the young man's arousal, Rick tugged gently as he lavished attention on the sensitive nipple.

"God, that feels bloody marvelous," Billy moaned.

"Hang on to your hat," Rick said. "I'm just getting warmed up."

Rick never gave the kid a chance to reciprocate as he swarmed over the superbly toned and tanned body, taking his pleasure in the responses he evoked. Used to being the provider, Billy relaxed for once and reveled in the role of receiver.

"Did Gareth ever touch you like this?" Rick asked.

For a second, the question shocked Billy out of his fevered state. Rick worked his fingertip a few millimeters deeper into the young man's tight sheathe and Billy whimpered his pleasure.

"No, Gareth never touched me like this," Billy said slowly and found the words didn't hurt nearly as much as he thought they would. "He was always rough, and he liked for me to pretend I didn't want to be touched. Forcing me got him hot; forcing me to take him without preparation really got him off."

"And did it get you off?" Rick asked as he circled the young man's prostate with a teasing fingertip.

"Ngh! God! You're driving me mad with that," Billy panted.

"Please answer the question, Mr. Rosen," Rick said flicking his tongue against a taut nipple.

"No!" Billy moaned. "It didn't get me off and it pissed him off that he couldn't make me cum while he was fucking me."

"There's nothing wrong with you," Rick said. "And I'm going to prove it to you now."

Billy's heart began to hammer as Rick knelt between his wide-flung legs. His breath came short and fast as strong hands grasped his hips and settled his buttocks on muscular thighs. Billy's bones melted as a hot hardness pressed against his cleft.

"Shit!" Rick hissed. "Hang on. I forgot about lube."

Billy groaned his disappointment as Rick lowered his leg to the mattress.

"Don't pout, tiger kitten. Try this."

A small clear plastic bag landed on the bed next to Billy as Rick spun toward the sound of the rich, familiar voice.

"That's pure cocaine," Gareth said. "It'll numb you up a treat and then Rick can tear up that tight little arse. Remember, sugar bum? All the fun we used to have?"

"No," Billy said, scrambling up. "You can't be here. You're dead. You're dead. You can't be here. You can't!"

"Whoa there, old son," Gareth said, leveling his gun at Rick.

Rick froze with one foot on the floor. "Can we put our pants on?"

"Negative," Gareth said. "Get back on the bed, stud. Billy, as you were."

"Fuck you," Billy responded instantly.

"You always get everything arse-backwards, kitten," Gareth sighed. "Now pick up that coke and use it or I'll blow Rick's willy off."

"Easy there," Rick said. "Let's take it down a notch, Elvis. Before anything else happens, will you tell me how you managed to get in here?"

His vanity touched, Gareth smirked at the cop. "It was quite easy actually. I stole an ambulance and drove right up to the police car at the top of the drive. It was a simple matter to shoot them as they got out to see how they could help me. This silencer is worth every penny it retails for."

Rick knew it was a mistake, but he had to ask. "And the guards in the house?"

"Mmm," Gareth purred. "I happened across a truly stunning dusky-skinned bird, and who do you think she was snogging? You can't imagine."

"A British cop named Campbell Frehley?" Rick said to keep Gareth talking.

"Oh. Well, it looks as though you can imagine. Speaking for myself, I was quite astounded I can tell you. It looks as though everyone that worked for me had a secret agenda. You and Paul are both coppers, Geordie was out for himself, and Billy...well, he's the biggest surprise of all."

"Fuck you," Billy said.

"Now you're just being repetitive," Gareth said, glancing at the young man, "and very tempting. Use the cocaine, Billy, unless you want me to apply it with the barrel of this gun. And be sparing, if you please. That's all that's left of my fortune."

"Are you deaf as well as daft?" Billy asked. "Fuck you, Gareth."

Gareth rolled his head on his neck. "You keep talking about fucking. Do you want me to fuck you, baby-snakes?"

"That's not going to happen," Rick heard himself say. "And his name is Billy."

"His name is whatever I say it is." Gareth pointed the gun at Rick again. "Did I mention that your partner is alive? She's tied up in the sitting room right now. I had to threaten Frehley's life to subdue her, but after I shot him the second time, she saw I meant business and settled right down."

Rick took a deep breath to steady his voice. "You know we check in with headquarters at regular intervals," he said.

"That's right, so we'd better get on with it. Make no mistake; I'm here for one thing. Vengeance. I'm going to make the two of you pay, and I don't give a shit what happens to me after that."

# ~ Chapter Nineteen ~

"HOW?" Billy asked his former employer. "How is it possible that you're here?"

Gareth chuckled. "You'll like this; it's ironic. I hooked up with Geordie when we were both cutting our teeth on the London drug scene. He was from the same area I was and just a few months older. It wasn't until some whore mentioned it that I noticed how much we looked alike and began using it to advantage. It comes in awfully handy when objective witnesses will swear they saw you in a bar while you were allegedly shooting some shite-for-brains dealer in another part of the city. Never thought Geordie would fuck me over like that, but I guess he got his instant karma for stealing the car from me."

"So it was Geordie in the car with the bomb, and you on the roof with the sniper rifle," Rick said.

"And Colonel Mustard in the library with the candlestick," Billy muttered.

Rick wished Billy would keep quiet as Gareth's eye fell on the young man again.

"You're quite a piece of work, my red angel," Gareth said. "It staggers me to think about it. You fucked your way to me just so you could kill me. And now that you think you've gotten away with it, and with a bonus boyfriend no less, I show up. What a burner on you, eh?"

"Yeah, but you're fucked, too, aren't you?" Billy said. "No money, no thugs, no blow."

"Keep talking, tiger kitten. You're making my payback sweeter with every word."

"Why don't you kill me or do whatever twisted thing you came here to do? Because I'm just bloody sick and tired of you."

"You are such a bitch," Gareth said, putting the hair up on Rick's neck. "You know, I stood at the door for a few minutes listening to you before I came in. I was a little offended by what you said."

"I can't imagine how I could care less," Billy said. "You're bad in bed, you arsehole. That's the truth, and I'll stand behind it."

Gareth smiled, his eyes glinting with nasty glee. "You're really getting me worked up, baby. The way only you can."

"Ah, fuck it," Rick said. "Kill me, if you want, but I can't listen to you talk to Billy like that anymore. It just turns my stomach."

Gareth rolled his eyes. "If it isn't Sir Galahad," he said. "Don't kid yourself, mate. Billy likes being treated like a whore. Now why don't you climb back on top of him and give him what he really wants."

"Not a chance," Rick said. "We're not going to perform for you."

"Why not?" Billy said unexpectedly. "Why don't you show this wanker how a real man makes love?"

Rick finally turned to look at the kid. Their eyes met and a silent message was exchanged. Rick nodded fractionally. He had to start trusting Billy sometime. "Sure," the undercover cop said. "If that's what you want."

Gareth gestured to the door with his gun. "I think it's what your partner would want," he said. "You can start fucking, or I can walk out there and shoot her in the head."

"Just for the record," Rick said. "How does forcing me to do Billy help you get satisfaction?"

"Here are the rules," Gareth said. "If Billy cums, I shoot you. If he doesn't, I shoot him. Understand?"

Rick took a second to appreciate the perverse cleverness of Gareth's scheme. "I don't think I can get hard again with that gun pointed at me."

"No one could," Billy said. "No one except for psychos like Gareth. Why do they gravitate toward me?"

"It's not your fault," Rick said.

"I love it," Gareth said. "It's not your fault. Say it enough times and it becomes the truth. Blame society. Blame your parents. Shite, blame me if you want to, but the truth is that Billy's a born whore."

"Rick, don't!" Billy cried out.

Rick froze in his tracks, but he didn't look at Billy. He continued to glare at Carey, his hands clenching and unclenching at his sides.

194

"Don't make him shoot you," Billy said. "I am a whore. Or I was, anyway. The truth doesn't hurt me."

"The hell it doesn't," Rick said. "The truth's the most painful thing I can think of."

"Enough of this sparkling banter," Gareth said. "I've changed my mind. Billy, tie Rick's hands with his belt. I think watching me fuck you will hurt him a lot more than a bullet in the gut."

"Finally you get down to the real reason you're here: your less than adequate dick."

"I will really miss you, mate," Gareth said. "However, Billy's tongue is just as sharp and he's prettier than you. No offense."

"No offense taken," Rick said. "Billy, do what he says, okay? Don't make him shoot you; promise me."

Billy nodded as he rose slowly, making a production of it. He slid languidly from the bed and sauntered across the room to pick up Rick's belt like one of Chippendales' finest. As Gareth's eyes tracked the sweet moves, Rick made one of his own. Surging up from the mattress, he launched himself at the armed man. Gareth saw the sudden motion in his peripheral vision and swung the gun around before he turned his head. He fired blindly and the round entered the wall three feet to Rick's right. Billy hit the drug lord from the side, as Gareth pulled the trigger again, and again the bullet went wide. Gareth landed hard with the kid uppermost and grabbing for the gun. Using his superior mass, Gareth rolled Billy beneath him. Rick grasped one of Gareth's shoulders and socked him hard on the jaw. The silenced weapon went off between Gareth and Billy, and Rick yanked harder, pulling the fugitive off the young man. Billy held fast to the weapon, as Gareth's finger tightened on the trigger. A round thunked into the carpet next to Billy's head, as Rick landed another blow, rocking Gareth and breaking two of Rick's fingers. Still, the gunman refused to go down. Wrapping his hands around Gareth's throat, Rick began to throttle him. Gareth tried to turn the gun on Rick, but Billy's grip remained firm. As his air ran out, the drug lord struggled frantically, but he was held in an unbreakable grip. After what seemed an eternity, Hairy Carey's eyes rolled up and he went limp. As the big man toppled, taking Rick with him, Paul Macross appeared in the doorway, gun drawn. He stared at the three entangled men and recognized Gareth.

"Fuck me!" Paul exclaimed. "It's Carey."

"Yeah," Rick said. "It turns out he's not entirely dead after all."

Paul came into the room and knelt to put cuffs on the unconscious Gareth. "I thought it was Geordie Cook."

"And I thought he killed you," Rick said.

"Kevlar, mate," Paul said, rapping his chest. "Been wearing it since Novacelli shot me."

"Smart man. Paul's a smart man, isn't he, Billy?"

Rick looked down and realized Billy was too still, and that there was far too much blood on and around him.

"Shit!" Rick said, touching the kid's cheek. "Billy!"

"Just a few more minutes, Mum," Billy mumbled. "And then I'll get up. Promise."

"Thank God," Rick said. "I thought you'd been shot."

Billy blinked and let Rick help him up. "No, I'm okay; just a little shaken. This is Gareth's blood."

Paul was already talking into his radio. In addition to the backup he'd called for when he came to, he arranged for an ambulance. The British agent stayed to guard Gareth while Rick and Billy went to check on the other people in the house. The two men found Graciela tied to a chair, inching her way to Campbell's body. Campbell lay in a distressingly wide pool of red on the living room floor, but he was breathing and had a pulse. Rick freed Graciela as Billy did what he could for Campbell. They could already hear the faint wailing of sirens as cruisers and rescue vehicles turned off the highway. In minutes, the house was teeming with official personnel that quickly, efficiently, and dispassionately took charge. Before those directly involved in the murder attempt had time to catch their breath, they found themselves hustled into ambulances.

Graciela insisted on riding with Inspector Frehley, but before the vehicle began to move, she made a sudden decision. With a last look at Campbell, so pale against the stretcher, she opened the rear door and jumped out. As she set off at a trot, she called back to the strapping EMT. "Take good care of him or it's your ass, *pendejo*."

The medic nodded and held up his hand in a pledge as he shut the doors. The siren wound up again, and the ambulance drove away, following the one that transported Rick and Billy. Graciela borrowed a riot gun from an unattended cruiser and approached the car that Gareth was in. As Graciela walked up, the young cop behind the wheel started the engine, but he didn't hit the lights and siren just yet. Politely, he rolled down his window and waited for her.

"Good evening, officer," Graciela said. "I see you have Mr. Carey in the backseat. I was wondering if I might have a word with him before you go."

The officer kept his head down, the brim of his cap shading his face as he answered. "Afraid I can't do that, ma'am," he said with a soft Latin accent. "My orders are to take care of him immediately."

"It's very important, *carnale*," she lowered her voice. "He tried to kill my partner."

"I understand, ma'am. Believe me, I do, but I can't allow you access to him. Now if you'll excuse me."

"I don't excuse you," Graciela said harshly, swinging the sawed-off shotgun up to point at the other officer. To her surprise, she was looking down the barrel of a very big bore gun. Carefully, she lowered hers and held her arms away from her body. "That's no cop's gun," she said.

"I'd appreciate it if you didn't let everybody else know right away," the imposter said. "And I promise not to drill a big hole in that gorgeous face of yours."

"*Chingate!*" Graciela swore. "You'll never get away with this, *cabron*. Even if you and Gareth get away, we'll find him again, and we'll find you, too."

"You got me all wrong, *chica*," the young man chuckled. "My name's Hector, but the ladies call me El Toro, and I don't work for Carey. I'm outside talent brought in by friends of the late, great Antonio Marcial."

Graciela's jaw dropped as Hector put the car in gear and drove away over the lawn until he reached the road. The cruiser picked up speed, its taillights disappearing down the tunnel of the trees. Graciela stood and watched in silence as the perp got away. When the police car turned onto the highway, Officer Cruz walked back to the house and made a preliminary report. Not once did she mention the strange officer that had taken Carey to be booked. She was concise and extremely brief and left as soon as possible for the hospital. Rick and Billy met Graciela in the emergency room waiting area and assured her that Campbell's chances were good. Apparently, Gareth was a very bad shot, as Billy had once observed. Relieved, Graciela ordered her partner to get some rest.

"Hold on a minute, detective," Captain Little said as he came through the door. "You're not in charge here. Not yet anyway. We can't just let Mr. Rosen go in Officer Miles' custody."

"Why not?" Graciela asked. "Carey's being incarcerated as we speak, so he's no longer a danger and…"

"Um, yeah," Walter Little said. "About that. It appears that one of our cruisers is missing and so is Gareth Carey. Two officers who were found unconscious at the safe house say that they were hit from behind while escorting Carey to the car. So it appears he had an accomplice we didn't know about."

"Call it a hunch," Graciela said, "but I don't think Gareth's going to bother us again."

"Your hunches notwithstanding," Little said, "I think I'll follow police procedure. As unfamiliar with it as you may be, I'm going to insist that you humor me and at least fake it."

"Whatever you say, captain," Rick answered, forestalling his partner's comment. "How soon can you get us to a new safe house?"

"I can answer that," Paul Macross said, as he joined them. "I've been on the phone for the last hour with my superiors back home and they've been on the phone with the higher-ups here in America. Your people are going to accept Billy and Rick's oral and written testimony in lieu of court appearances."

"Why would they do that?" Little asked.

"Because when Gareth Carey is caught, he'll be extradited to England to stand trial for the murder of DCI Arthur Oldham. Billy was the only witness to the crime, so we'll need him over there. I just received permission to book a flight."

"When?" Billy asked.

"As soon as we can get to the airport," Paul told him. "The sooner you're away from here, the safer you'll be."

Billy turned to look at Rick, more panicked than he'd been the entire time his life was in danger. Rick closed his hand reassuringly over Billy's cold fingers and addressed Paul and Walter.

"Billy's not going anywhere without me," he said.

"Then I guess I'd better book another ticket," Paul said without blinking.

As the Brit took out his cell phone and considerately walked out of the waiting area, Captain Little gave Rick a stern look.

"Have you thought about this?" the captain asked.

"I have," Rick said. "If leaving now means I lose my job, then so be it."

"That's too bad," Little said. "I hate to lose a good cop like you."

Rick's throat grew suddenly tight, making it hard to speak. "It means a lot to me that you think I'm a good cop," he said. "But I'm beginning to think that my place isn't on the force."

"There are a lot of other ways to fight crime," Graciela said softly.

"Hey," Rick said. "I know this comes as a complete surprise, but…"

"No it doesn't," she said. "I've always known you were a romantic. Follow your heart, *hermano*. It's your best destiny."

Rick swept his partner up from the uncomfortable plastic chair and into his very comfortable embrace. Graciela hugged him back fiercely, whispering in his ear as they clung together for several long moments. When Rick released her and stepped back, he winked before kissing her goodbye. The captain shook Rick's hand and Billy hugged Graciela as Paul came to collect his charge. Paul shook Walter's hand as well and promised to stay in constant touch; Campbell was still in surgery, and Paul was anxious for updates. Looking nervous, but determined in his first outing as team leader, Paul shepherded Rick and Billy out of the hospital.

Less than an hour later, they were sitting in the first-class cabin of a 707-jetliner bound for their layover in New York City, before they traveled on to London. Paul had impressed upon the flight attendants the need for discretion and privacy. He was assured that no one would bother him and his companions unless the call button was pushed.

"Yuck," Billy said succinctly. "I feel as if I've been wearing these clothes all my life."

"I hear you," Rick said, getting settled in the very comfortable seat and raising the arm that separated his chair from Billy's. "I must smell like the monkey cage at the zoo."

Billy put his head on Rick's shoulder and sniffed audibly. "You smell sexy," he said.

"You're deluded," Rick answered. "But I love you and I'm looking forward to finishing what we started."

"There's always the mile-high club," Billy suggested.

"I'm afraid that would put me in the six-feet-under club right now," Rick answered. "And anything good is worth waiting for."

"I can't believe what a square you turned out to be." Billy smiled. "I remember my first sight of you in those tight leather pants, all golden and glowering, like a rogue lion on the prowl. Talk about lies in advertising."

"I am a rogue lion on the prowl, babe," Rick said. "But it's a fact that lions spend most of their time sleeping."

"True," Billy conceded, as Rick's arm settled around his shoulders and pulled him closer. "What do you suppose lions dream about?" he asked drowsily.

"I know what square lions dream about," Rick said, his lips brushing Billy's forehead.

"I like squares," Billy said. "If they come equipped with long round pegs." Fetching a deep sigh, the young man spoke again, his voice blurry with exhaustion. "What do square lions dream about?"

"Their mates, of course," Rick murmured. "Square lions are monogamous."

"I wanna be a square—." Billy dropped off to sleep in midsentence.

Rick smiled and levered his seat back a little farther. Billy snuggled closer and Rick's arms tightened around the young man. Resting his cheek on top of Billy's head, the soon-to-be ex-cop watched the sky get lighter as they flew toward the sun, until he couldn't stay awake any longer. As his eyes shut and stayed that way, he gave thanks that he had someone to fall asleep with.

# ~ *Epilogue* ~

Rick kicked at the emerald turf, scattering crystal droplets from the drizzle that had freighted the breeze all morning. There was a chill in the English spring air that wasn't present in Southern California even in winter, but Rick was well armored against the bone-deep damp that pervaded everything. Lifting his gaze from the ground, the ex-cop found the only warm spot in the day.

Billy stood about fifty feet away with his hands in the pockets of his long coat, newly shorn hair plastered to his cheeks and forehead in dark commas. His fingers rested lightly on the top curve of a sparsely decorated monument. As his lips moved in words Rick could not hear, Billy absently stroked the polished stone.

"They found his body and identified the pieces a few hours after we landed at Gatwick," Billy was saying. "Whatever Gareth may have done in his misbegotten life, I'm not sure anyone deserves to go like that. I guess I've lost my stomach for vengeance if I can pity him. Anyway, I thought you'd like to know that it's really over. I probably won't be coming here as much now, but I think you'll be pleased at the reason. I brought a Yank back with me, and he seems awfully keen. He reminds me so much of you that sometimes I expect him to speak with your brogue. He's not you though," Billy drew his sleeve quickly across his eyes and took a shaky breath. "And I'm glad. I'll always love you, Arthur, but I know now that you were just trying to help a lost boy. You could never have seen me as a lover. It's no one's fault. It's just the way the world made us." Billy glanced over his shoulder at Rick and then back down at the name and the dates carved into the granite. "I'm sorry, Arthur," the young man said. "I wish you had lived. I would have liked Rick to meet you. This is the best I can do: I promise never to do anything you would be ashamed of. Goodbye, Arthur. I'll never forget you."

Billy turned from Arthur's grave and walked purposefully toward Rick. Rick put his arm around the young man's shoulders and Billy put his around Rick's waist, as they kept moving toward the car. Quickly getting inside the big sedan, they reveled in the warm air blowing out of the vents.

"Did you say what you needed to?" Rick asked.

Billy nodded. "It's been a weird forty-eight hours," he said. "The only sleep we've had was on the plane."

"We've organized accommodations for you," Paul Macross said from the front seat. "Inspector Frehley is already trying to run things from a hospital bed in America, but I prevailed on this one. If you're ready, PC Parker will drive us to the rooms I booked."

"You just got my vote," Rick said, sitting back against the tobacco-brown leather as the big car moved into the stream of traffic.

In one of the oldest districts of the city, the officer coasted to a stop in the courtyard of a venerable U-shaped stone building. PC Parker got out and opened the door on Rick's side.

"Where are we?" Billy mumbled, raising his head from Rick's shoulder.

"This was an abbey until the fourteenth century," Paul said. "It's been a few things since, but now it's a bed-and-breakfast. Just go through the gate. Here's the key to cottage number four. It's all arranged."

"Thank you," Billy said, holding out his hand.

Paul took the young man's hand and pulled him into a hug.

"You really gave me a hard time, Mr. Willem Rosen," Paul said.

"I spared no one," Billy answered. "I was an awful pill."

"No argument there, mate." Paul grinned as he held out a hand to Rick.

Rick hugged Paul, thanking him for the million and one strings Rick knew Paul must have pulled to make things so smooth for him and Billy.

"Look me up if you want a job," Paul said as he got back in the car.

"Anything's possible," Rick said, as he walked away with Billy.

"Alone at last," Billy said as they crossed the lovely formal garden to the sweet little stone cottage with an ornately embellished number four painted on the door. Within they found the space divided into a sitting room, bedroom, and small bath with a fire already lit in the hearth. The bathroom was stocked with toiletries, to Billy's delight. "I'm having a quick bath and shave," the young man said from the doorway.

Rick walked over and enveloped Billy in his embrace. "Of course you are," he said. "But first, I'm going to get you good and dirty."

"No!" Billy protested, pulling away. "I need to be clean before we start."

"No you don't," Rick disagreed. "Despite my words, there's nothing dirty about making love, babe. And you don't need to be scrubbed and perfumed to attract me. I won't be put off by your sweat, or anything else that comes out of you. When I said I loved you, I meant all of you, not just the nice bits."

"Are you saying there are bits of me that aren't nice?"

"Well, maybe one or two," Rick teased.

"Point them out," Billy said. "I'm totally into self-improvement."

"I'll have to take your clothes off first."

"I was going to take them off anyway. I don't normally bathe in my clothes."

"Smartass."

"Well then, I guess that's one area that's nice enough already."

"From what I've seen, it's outstanding," Rick said, working buttons and zippers until Billy stood naked in front of him.

"Outstanding?" Billy raised an eyebrow.

"Outstanding," Rick confirmed, turning Billy away from him to inspect closely the area under discussion. "And that's official."

"Mmm," Billy purred as Rick caressed his nether cheeks. "Is that the Frederick Miles Feel of Approval?"

"That's right," Rick said, his voice muffled as he pulled his shirt over his head. "And I intend to put my mark on every square inch of you."

"Square inches for a square lion?" Billy asked, as Rick's jeans hit the floor.

"You remember that?" Rick asked as he slotted his arousal in the downy valley of Billy's buttocks. "I thought you were asleep."

"Let that be a warning to you," Billy said as he pushed back against Rick's hardness. "I hear you even in my sleep, so you'd better be nice."

"It's *your* niceness that's up for debate," Rick reminded as he brushed his lips along one smooth shoulder. "But I find your arguments more than persuasive."

"Mmm, that's nice," Billy said as Rick nipped at his nape. "So you find me persuasive?"

"I find most of you to be downright seductive, irresistible even."

Billy hummed softly as a warm tongue traced the whorls of his ear. Rick plucked gently at the young man's nipples, coaxing them to blunt points. Nibbling at Billy's earlobe, Rick slid his hands slowly down to rest on either side of his lover's rising flesh. Flattening his palms against the silky skin, Rick stroked the creases of Billy's groin and thighs while pressing him firmly backward.

"You are getting me incredibly hot," Billy murmured over his shoulder.

Craning his neck, Rick captured the young man's lips in an awkward but passionate kiss. Billy gave Rick his mouth, opening to him in utter trust. As the kiss deepened, one of Rick's arms went around Billy's chest while his other hand nestled possessively at Billy's crotch. Billy whimpered into the other man's mouth as his stiffening cock was fondled ardently.

"I'm not complaining, but could we take this to the bed?" Billy asked breathlessly. "My knees are going to give out soon."

"I'd catch you, babe," Rick said. "But if you're ready for bed, I'm not gonna argue."

"One second," Billy said. "First, let's find something we can use for lube. Remember what happened last time you stopped to look for it?"

"That's not funny," Rick said.

"No, it bloody well isn't," Billy said. "So start searching, detective."

Rick swung Billy around in his arms and deposited him on the mattress before going into the bathroom. Billy could hear the man opening the cabinet and moving bottles on the shelves. In less than a minute, Rick returned holding a tube as though it were Excalibur.

"I take it that's not toothpaste," Billy quipped.

"Try Liqui-Silk Ultra-Glide Premium Personal Lubricant Gel," Rick said.

Billy chuckled. "Paul thinks of everything, it would seem."

"Unless…. You don't think one of the monks left this behind, do you?"

"Give me that," Billy said. "If you're just going to play with it, I'll hold onto it."

Rick set the tube on the nightstand and stretched out on his side next to Billy. "Does it bother you to hear how beautiful you are?" he asked.

"No. Does it bother you?"

"I'm not beautiful," Rick scoffed, trailing his fingers down Billy's long thighs.

"You most certainly are," Billy said with feeling. "Have you ever looked in a mirror? You're gorgeous and you're dead sexy. My God, your eyes alone make you more beautiful than most men. And those cheekbones…"

"All right," Rick said. "That's enough of that."

"So it does bother you," Billy said gleefully.

"I didn't say that," Rick said, ruffling the dark curls around the young man's arousal with his breath.

"Rick?"

"Yep."

"I'm all for letting you take the lead, but could we get on with it? I need to feel your hands on me."

Rick looked up into Billy's eyes and a spark jumped the gap between them. Though Rick had resolved that their first time making love would be a gentle, slow-paced experience, he found his impatience matched the other man's. All he could think of was plunging his aching arousal into Billy's heat.

"Yes," Billy sighed happily, as Rick took his mouth in no uncertain manner.

Rick's hands were everywhere, setting small fires that quickly blazed out of control until they merged into one great conflagration of pleasure. Rick moaned as the young man found his shaft and caressed him skillfully. The long cool fingers stroked and fondled the ex-cop's straining cock, the weighty sack and moist cleft as the kiss went on. Rick was reluctant to leave the sweet mouth, but he kissed his way down the Brit's long neck to his smooth chest. Billy lost contact with Rick's groin and whined his displeasure as he started to rise. Rick threw a leg over Billy, pinning him as he lowered his mouth to tongue the young man's nipples in turn. Billy's complaint ceased for lack of breath. Rick had stolen it with his knowledge of erogenous zones. Billy panted, moaned, and cried out Rick's name as the man caressed him to a fever pitch of excitement.

"Let me…" Billy said, as Rick slid lower.

"Shhh," Rick said. "I'm finishing what I started back at the safe house. I'm doing this because I want to. I don't expect anything from you in return. Understand? You don't have to touch me unless you want to. I'm going to do my best to get you off, but if you don't cum, that's okay. I'll still enjoy what I'm about to do."

Rick squirted some of the clear, sweet-smelling lubricant on his fingers and prodded delicately at Billy's entrance. Billy spread his legs wider, and reached down to stroke Rick's hair as the man put his cheek against the flat belly. Rick drew the head of Billy's arousal into his mouth, swirling his tongue around the tip as he sucked gently. Billy held his breath as the teasing finger eased into him. Deftly, Rick found the slight swelling in the front wall of the resilient sheath. Rubbing firmly in figure eights, Rick stimulated the small gland as he bobbed his head on Billy's shaft. Billy clutched at the sheets as the tension in his groin wound tighter and tighter. He had been here before, perched on this pinnacle, waiting to fly, but it rarely happened. It usually ended in frustration and a dull ache in his balls.

"It's okay," Rick said, relinquishing the stiff rod. "You can relax. I really don't care if you cum or not. I just want to suck your beautiful dick and move my fingers around inside you."

"You're insane," Billy murmured.

"Possibly, but not because I want to make love to you," Rick replied. "Seriously. Do whatever you want. I'm just going to go back to what I was doing."

Billy gasped as a second finger joined the first and Rick engulfed his hard length down to the root. Eagerly, with all evidence of pleasure, Rick lavished attention on Billy's cock, balls, perineum, and prostate. The young man was in a delirium of sensual bliss, giving himself freely for the first time.

"Oh God!" Billy exclaimed as the coil of spiraling sensation reached a point where he felt as though he would snap if it didn't stop. "God! Please! Rick! I can't..." Abruptly, Billy went utterly still. Then he sucked in a big breath and let it out in an abandoned cry of release. Rick continued to stroke the young man's sweet spot as he swallowed the cum jetting from Billy's cock. Letting the sated rod slide from between his lips, Rick withdrew his fingers from the clenching sheath and put his arms around his lover's waist. "Bloody hell," Billy said in a shaky voice. "You've cured me, mate."

Rick snuggled his face into the young man's quivering abdomen. "Nah. You came because you wanted to."

"You make me want to cum," Billy said, stroking Rick's hair. "I'm not an object like a toy or a trophy to you."

"You were something of an obstacle for a while though."

"Shut up!"

"You sound like you've recovered. Ready for more?"

"I'm ready for your cock," Billy said. "You've deprived me for too long."

"I guess this would be the optimum time," Rick mused. "You're lubed up, stretched a little, and all relaxed in the afterglow. Really no reason why we…"

"Rick, please!" Billy interrupted. "Just give it to me. Now!"

"Spoiled brat," Rick commented as he moved between the tanned thighs.

"Who just spoiled me for all other men?" Billy countered.

"Yeah, you say that now." Rick continued talking to cover his sudden nervousness. "What if I'm a lousy cocksman?"

"Cocksman? Is that a real word?" Billy asked.

"Pretty sure it is," Rick said as he slicked his arousal.

"Sounds like you made it up," Billy said, as the blunt head of Rick's shaft pressed against his opening. "Then again…. Cocksman. Hmm. I like it."

Rick leaned forward slightly, lifting one of Billy's legs to his shoulder. The tip of his rock-hard dick entered the tight channel.

"Oh God…yes!" Billy gasped. "I like it a lot!"

"Let me know if I go too fast, or…"

"It's fine. I'm fine. You're fine. Everything's fine. It's fantastic, in fact! Go for it!"

"Easy, there," Rick smiled. "Don't forget; I'm injured."

"Poor baby," Billy said with less than convincing sincerity. "I'm not wounded and I can take it. You don't have to coddle me."

"I want to," Rick said, sliding forward another inch. "I know you can take it, but why should you have to? This isn't about me pounding away at you until I shoot my wad. If you're not enjoying it, I won't be able to either."

"Are you joking?" Billy said incredulously.

"Nope. That's my kink. I can't get off unless my lover does."

"Mate, this has to be a dream," Billy said.

"I was just thinking the same thing," Rick said as he passed the halfway mark and Billy bore down on him. "Holy shit! That feels amazing."

Billy smiled languidly. "If you like that," he said, "you'll love this."

Rick gasped as Billy planted the soles of his feet against the mattress, clenched his opening, and took in the rest of Rick's shaft. Rick's head dropped back and he let out his breath in a groan of intense pleasure as the ring of muscle flexed on the thick base of his cock. "Wow!" Rick breathed.

"That's just the tip of the iceberg," Billy said. "You're on my playing field now and I intend to show you all my flashiest moves."

"Not all at once, I hope," Rick said. "I'm not sure my heart could take it."

Billy laughed and Rick's heart opened like a rose at the carefree sound. There were no shadows in Billy's eyes just now; the young man's gaze sparkled with humor, with desire, and with hope. With the same light, in fact, that illuminated Rick's eyes.

Leaning in, Rick bent his lover's limber body to capture the sweetly curved lips. With a kiss that was almost chaste in its reverence, he rocked gently in the velvet sheath. Small whimpers escaped Billy's throat to be muffled by Rick's mouth. Parting with Billy's alluring lips for the moment, Rick straightened, wrapping an arm around the leg that rested on his shoulder. Nuzzling the inside of Billy's knee, Rick pushed the young man's opposite leg flat against the mattress and watched his arousal sliding in and out.

"You really are astonishingly beautiful," Rick said softly.

"If that pleases you, I'm happy to be beautiful for you," Billy said in a strained voice.

Rick pulled back until only the tip of his shaft was still sheathed. Grasping Billy's lolling cock, Rick thrust in steady, shallow strokes. Billy lifted his buttocks, changing the tilt of his pelvis, and Rick took the hint. Angling his thrust to the right, Rick dragged the head of his shaft over his lover's prostate.

"Just a…little…faster," Billy panted, moving his hips in concert with Rick's cadence.

Rick complied gladly and was rewarded by the young man's yelp of bliss. Warm, thick liquid spilled over Rick's knuckles as Billy shuddered through a profound orgasm.

"I don't...don't believe it," Billy stammered. "I never..."

Rick grinned as he increased the speed and depth of his stroke, pulling Billy's buttocks higher on his thighs. Billy opened his eyes and saw the joyous expression on his lover's handsome face. Returning the smile, Billy arched his back, rising with the ease and grace of a gymnast to straddle Rick. Rick leaned back as Billy crouched over him, posting on the hard rod of flesh. Billy took one pink nipple between his teeth and the other between thumb and forefinger as he rode the other man mercilessly. Rick groaned deep in his chest as Billy reached under him to tease his opening. In the next moment, Rick's release broke over him like a perfect wave, cresting, crashing, and foaming through him. Wrapping his arms around Billy, Rick rolled to the side, still ensconced, and pressed moist little kisses on every inch of skin he could comfortably reach. Billy all but purred contentedly in the shelter of Rick's arms, as they caught their breath. Brushing the hair away from Billy's damp forehead, Rick looked into his lover's eyes.

"I think this is going to work," he said.

The grainy, sated sound of the man's voice sent tingles skittering along Billy's nerve endings and he moved restlessly. Rick shifted a bit and prepared to pull out.

"Sorry," he said. "I kind of forgot I was still in the saddle."

Billy whined in protest and wrapped his long legs around Rick's hips. "Stay," he said. "And keep talking. I'm not uncomfortable and I like what the sound of your voice does to me."

"You want to go again?" Rick asked. "I'm a little tapped out right this second, but give me a minute and I'll see what I can do."

Billy's lips curled in a fond smile. "I'm fine. I want to lay here in your arms, connected to you, and just be still for a while."

"You've been on the move for a long time, huh?" Rick nuzzled the young man's neck.

"A lifetime," Billy said. "But I feel like I could settle now."

"Like...you want a home, and all that?"

"Yeah, that's what I mean. I don't need anything but you. I'd live in the streets again, if only you were there with me. I'd give up whatever you asked me to just to be with you. It's a little scary how much I need you, but, yeah, I want the cottage and the bed of roses and everything."

"You don't have to be scared. I won't leave you, and I won't let anyone take you away from me. That's a promise."

Billy took Rick's hand in his and held it over his heart. "I promise too," he said drowsily. "Forever and ever."

"I'd show you how happy that makes me if I wasn't falling asleep."

Billy laughed softly. "We're both knackered," he said. "I can't believe I'm still making sense. I'll let you sleep in a minute."

"I could listen to you talk for hours in that creamy, dreamy accent," Rick said, laying back and pulling Billy closer.

Billy snuggled in, putting an arm around Rick's chest and throwing a leg over him. "It reminds me of this poem that was one of

Arthur's favorites. I thought it was unbelievably sad and I couldn't understand why he liked it so much. I'm sure you know it; it's that one by Frost. The one about stopping near the woods in the snow."

"Yeah, sure," Rick rasped. "'The woods are lovely, dark and deep. But I have promises to keep, and miles to go before I sleep.'"

"And miles to go before I sleep," Billy said drowsily. "Isn't that sad?"

"I know you kept a hard promise, babe," Rick said in his lover's ear. "But it's over. You can sleep now and when you wake up, I'll be right here."

Billy's eyes were closed, but his lips curved up in a smile so sweet that Rick had to kiss him just one more time. Billy drifted off and Rick was not far behind. The ex-police officer's mind was filled with a torrent of possibilities, but he stemmed the tide for the time being. Plans could wait; right now, he was happy. With his arms and his heart full, Rick let sleep take him.

And as he slept, he dreamed of a cottage in winter, its windows alight with a buttery glow as he tramped home through the snow. In the open door, his lover stood with arms spread wide in welcome. Dropping his burdens, Rick ran toward his happiness.

## CONNIE BAILEY

I was born on an Air Force base and I've been in flight ever since. My father took the family with him wherever he was stationed; Spain, Morocco, Turkey, and Alaska were among his postings. While studying commercial arts, I married a musician who turned out to be a pilot in disguise. Having no burning ambition of my own at the time, I devoted myself to his dream. His job as aircraft designer and competition pilot has taken us all over the world. I have now set foot on almost every continent (a personal life ambition), but I don't hold out much hope for Antarctica anymore.

I have always loved to read. Since I was four, reading has been my favorite diversion and books my best friends. A few years ago, with my husband's support, I set out to become a writer. I wrote every day and posted what I wrote at various Internet groups and later on livejournal. I cannot recommend this school of writing highly enough. The candid feedback I received was invaluable to my development. I kept working at it, and one day I received the most exciting e-mail ever. A publisher wanted to talk to me.

That's pretty much it so far. There are a few fun facts like: my only child is a rescued Greyhound named Lizard, I live at a small grass airfield with a hang gliding school, I have what's commonly referred to as a "photographic memory", I collect words as a hobby, and my only nickname is "The Judge".

Connie Bailey

www.ingramcontent.com/pod-product-compliance
Lightning Source LLC
Chambersburg PA
CBHW051645260626
47170CB00004B/1352